No Ho...

Although not originally intent on becoming a children's author, Geoffrey Trease, born in 1909, has always loved writing and history, and was able to combine the two in his first children's novel – *Bows Against the Barons*, published in 1934. Since then he has written some eighty books for children and a number of adult works, including novels and a history of London. His works have appeared in twenty-six countries and twenty languages. Many were dramatized as radio serials in the old BBC's *Children's Hour*.

Geoffrey Trease has travelled widely in Europe, lived in Russia and served in India in the Second World War. He now lives in Bath, where his daughter, Jocelyn, is a college lecturer – with the happy result that he thus maintains constant touch with his four granddaughters and his great grand-children.

NO HORN AT MIDNIGHT

Geoffrey Trease

MACMILLAN
CHILDREN'S BOOKS

First published 1995 by Pan Macmillan Children's Books

This edition published 1995 by Macmillan Children's Books,
a division of Macmillan Publishers Limited
25 Eccleston Place, London SW1W 9NF
and Basingstoke

Associated companies throughout the world

ISBN 0 330 34141 3

1 3 5 7 9 8 6 4 2

A CIP catalogue record for this book is available
from the British Library

Phototypset by Intype, London
Printed by Mackays of Chatham, Kent

For another William

I

Ten ravenous passengers got stiffly down from the coach in the dawn light. Exactly twenty minutes later (for post office regulations were unyielding) only nine men swallowed a final mouthful and clambered aboard again. In the feverish bustle William had been concentrating too hard on his duties to notice that discrepancy. When he did so, he could not have foreseen that so trivial a fact was to affect the future of the whole town. Nobody's more than his own.

The coach had clattered away down the street with a farewell blast on the guard's long horn. The solitary figure at the table was finishing his meal with leisurely enjoyment. So, thought William, thank God the gentleman had not been left behind by accident. His father called softly from the doorway of the coffee-room.

'When Mr Holtby is ready, show him up to Number Six. His bags are at the foot of the stairs.'

'I will, Dad.'

His father went, moving with his usual quiet dignity. Before taking over the inn he had been butler in a great Yorkshire house and still looked it with his smooth moon face, sleek black hair and elegantly curving mutton-chop whiskers. William's mother had been cook in the same grand establishment. It was no wonder that when they

I

married and took over the Coach and Horses at Redford they made its high standards famous among the inns of northern England.

The stranger stood up, wiping his lips. 'I am ready now.' A southerner, from his quiet voice. A countryman perhaps? No pallid town-dweller. His lean face was bronzed. Even after the night journey his grey eyes were keen. With the ever-changing flow of new faces through the inn William was learning to observe people and sum them up.

He seized Mr Holtby's two bags, one rather weighty. Now that he had left school little allowance was made for his age and he was expected to tackle anything. Tight-lipped, he marched upstairs, pushed the door open with his elbow and stood aside. 'Number Six, sir.'

'A fair-sized table! Good.'

William misunderstood. 'Will you be requiring meals served in your room, sir?'

'Heavens, no! I'm used to eating anywhere. This candle's more to the point. I need a good light. Excellent.'

'Would you like a can of hot water now, sir?'

'Later.' Mr Holtby removed his watch and chain. 'Let us say at eight o'clock. I shall sleep for a couple of hours.'

Two hours did not sound much after a night on the road. 'If you were sound asleep, sir, would you wish the maid to rouse you, or – '

'She'll have no need. If I tell myself to wake at eight, I shall. Discipline,' said the stranger with a smile. He sat down and stretched out his legs. 'You might pull my boots off and take them down for cleaning.'

William knelt and tugged. Mr Holtby was not a young man – his hair was flecked iron-grey – but he was of a spare, athletic build. There was no sign of a pot belly under his elegant flowered waistcoat. William stood up, dangling the boots.

'Will that be all, sir?'

'Yes.' The man added casually: 'Would you be William?'

'Yes, sir.' He was mildly surprised that Mr Holtby had already picked up his name, but he seemed to be an observant type.

'Then we shall meet again.'

That could mean anything or nothing, but he was not left long in ignorance.

He joined the family at breakfast, one of the few times they usually managed to get together. Mostly they were hard at it, his mother in the kitchen, Frederick out in the stables, his father everywhere, himself anywhere that a job was given him. Redford was a staging post. Fifteen coaches a day in summer. That meant sixty horses to have ready for the road, sixty others to feed and water, maybe a hundred and fifty passengers to be served with a hot meal at lightning speed, never mind the rest of a big inn's general trade.

'Mr Holtby wants a guide for the moors,' said Mr Thornton. 'I told him you were just the lad. I said you knew the country round here like the back of your hand.'

William's spirits rose. His father's good opinion was welcome. Even more so was a day's escape from the humdrum jobs that were generally given him. He did

3

know the wild uplands around Redford. With two or three schoolfriends he had explored most of them.

'I'll pack a cold luncheon for the gentleman,' said his mother, 'and a bite for yourself. You'd better put on a clean neckcloth.'

'And wear a waistcoat,' said his father.

'Oh, Dad, it'll be scorching hot up there!'

'You're not just any lad from the yard, you're my son. You must be turned out respectable. But if he gives you anything for your trouble you can keep it,' Mr Thornton conceded. 'Only mind you tell me, so that I don't charge for your services on the bill.'

'Why shouldn't you?' said Frederick. 'If he chooses to give William something for himself as well, it's no concern of ours.'

'I'll charge no one twice for the same thing.'

'It's only business practice,' said Frederick sulkily.

'Not mine. You are not the keeper of this inn – yet.'

The awkward silence was broken by the distant horn of a mail approaching the tollgate at the entrance to the town. Mail coaches paid no tolls. It was a signal to the turnpike keeper to open his gate so that the team could come spanking through without slackening speed. Equally it was a warning to the ostlers to have four fresh horses standing ready in the yard. Frederick seized the chance to hurry off to his duties.

William was similarly well trained in punctuality. He was waiting when Mr Holtby came down at half-past eight, brisk and bright-eyed, chin smoothly shaven. Apart from the flowered waistcoat he had changed completely –

he might have been going out shooting in those grey breeches and brown leather leggings with his heavy square-toed boots. Only he would not have been shooting on the moors unless he was the Duke's guest, staying at the Castle, and it was too early for the season anyway. He had changed his top hat for a soft grey cap with a peak. Catching William's eye he smiled and said: 'High hats go badly with high winds in high places!'

'Yes, sir. It's always blowing up there.'

Mr Holtby wanted only a cup of coffee. He had seen the lunch basket. 'You've got the rations? Good. So it's all present and correct?'

'Yes, sir.'

'You might carry this for me as well.'

He handed William a soft oblong satchel of well-worn leather. The contents felt hard to the fingertips. Books perhaps, thought William. Was Mr Holtby planning to sit on the moors and *read*? William had never been a great reader. There was something intriguing about this stranger.

'Which way do you want to go, sir? Anywhere special you want to see?'

'Isn't there a high point called White Horse Edge? And Madwoman's Stones? Fascinating names you have hereabouts! Dead Man's Hill?' For a stranger Mr Holtby seemed surprisingly familiar with the local landmarks. 'And Lost Lass? If you can find *her* for me?' he added with a laugh.

'I can point out the moor, sir, but not the lass. She was a poor farm girl, a hundred years back. Took a short cut in a blinding snowstorm. Never seen again till spring when the drifts melted.' As Mr Holtby had set down his coffee-cup William seized the lunch basket and they started out.

Their way led along the High Street, across the cobbled square with its pillared market-house, and up the hill. He pointed out the church and the ancient grammar school he had left at Easter. Mr Holtby seemed interested in everything.

'Were you sorry to leave?'

William made a face. 'Not all that. Mr Melrose flogged you if you got low marks.'

'And did *you* get low marks?'

'At Latin grammar I did. Old Rosie thought it was all that mattered in life.'

'You disagreed?'

'I preferred mathematics.' He did not want to be set down as a dunce.

'More use in real life.' Mr Holtby sounded approving.

'I don't know, sir. Not much call for mathematics at an inn. There's only reckoning up the bills and so on.'

'Little scope for Euclid and his angles!'

'No. I did quite like geometry.'

'But you're working at the inn now? Following in your father's footsteps?'

'Just for now. If I wanted to do something different Dad wouldn't stand in my way. My elder brother will take over the inn when Dad gives up.' Better, he thought, to say no more.

He did not look forward to the day when he would be working under Fred's orders. Fred had ideas very different from their father's, very different from William's own.

Fortunately they were over the crest of the hill now and the whole moorland landscape rolled in front of them. Mr Holtby's interest shifted instantly to the view. He named landmarks before William could point them out. It was almost uncanny. Had the man really not been here before?

The hard road had petered out behind them. It was little more than a track used for driving the flocks up to the high pastures and down again, according to the season. It would have been narrower and fainter but for the occasional cart or sledge transporting peat from the bog. To get the best view William led the way up a steep heathery slope to the cluster of weird, weather-fashioned rocks named after the unknown Mad Woman.

The town had vanished below them. Except for their own soft footsteps and panting breath there was no sound but the drone of insects and the plaintive cries of the curlews, curl-*wee*, curl-*wee*, fading into the distance.

They reached the summit. 'A fine view, sir,' William gasped.

'It is indeed.'

They could see where the Pennine foothills dropped into the haze-hung Vale of York. 'On a clearer day,' said William, 'we'd see the Minster.' He indicated other landmarks.

Was Mr Holtby even listening? He murmured 'ah' or 'yes' but it sounded sometimes more like an answer to his own thoughts. He said abruptly: 'Excellent. I think we might move on.'

They swung west. 'The hill on the left is Dagger Stones, sir. Lost Lass is the much higher one to the right.'

'So the gap between – '

'Leads on to Cragdale Heights. And *they'll* give you a grand view of White Beacon Hags.'

Mr Holtby pounced on the name, which had already cropped up in their talk about the number of such names in the district. William had explained that these 'hags' were not more mad women or witches, but a local term for the gaps in a long cliff of limestone.

'But they're on the opposite side of Cragdale?'

'Yes, sir. But if we get up on the Heights we can see them facing us across the valley.'

'We'll do that, then.'

It looked an easy walk through the gap, two miles of almost level ground. 'But,' William warned him, 'we'd best stay on the higher slopes. Under Dagger Stones, yonder.'

'Why?'

'Down there it's mostly Featherbed Moss. And saying goes, "who lies down in Featherbed will never get up again".'

'Peat bog?' Mr Holtby was disappointingly matter-of-fact.

'Terribly deep, sir! Swallow a horse and man.'

'I know. I'd like to take a look at Featherbed Moss.'

William thought that they could see all they wanted to from where they were standing. But there was no telling with these gentlemen who came to visit the moors,

8

especially those who came alone. Perhaps Mr Holtby was interested in the wonders of nature, rare plants or butterflies or suchlike things. That might explain the book and whatever else he carried in the satchel.

The man was already plunging down the slope. William followed hastily. He had given him fair warning, and it was quite safe, with common sense, to approach the great swamp. But, as the guide, William knew he had the responsibility.

'Careful, sir!'

Mr Holtby had taken several experimental steps into the bog, prodding ahead of him with his stick. The brown peaty water was already bubbling up around his boot-tops. William hoped anxiously that he would not step too far and fall on his face. He wondered if he would have the strength to drag him back to safety. There was no help to run for in this desolate wilderness.

A curlew rose suddenly, noisily, from a clump of reeds Mr Holtby was approaching. Startled, Mr Holtby swore as his stick spun out of his hand. He moved to recover it, and cried out again in anger as the water washed higher up his legs. The stick still eluded him, lying flat on the spongy surface of the bog a few feet away.

'Leave it, sir!' Fear gave William's yell an accent of command. 'Stand where you are!' Mr Holtby stood, docile. Only the bubbles moved, sinister, around his knees.

William put down satchel and basket. He peeled off his jacket. He himself had no stick to hold out to the man and he could think of no better idea. If he held out the jacket at arm's length, and flapped it near enough for

Mr Holtby to catch hold, it might serve as well. If he waded too far into the bog himself he would be equally helpless.

Oh, thank *God*! Mr Holtby kept cool. At the second flap of the garment he caught the hem lightly between finger and thumb, and changed that hold into a firm two-handed grip.

'Hang on tight,' he said calmly, resuming command of the situation. 'But on no account let me pull you over. We don't want two of us! If you feel yourself going you *must* let go. Understand?'

'Yes, sir.'

'Good lad. We'll see now.'

With obvious effort he was dragging one leg out of the slime that sucked it back.

'Good,' he said between clenched teeth. The jacket sagged slack between them for a moment till William gathered it tighter. It was the life-and-death rope in a grim tug-of-war with himself and Mr Holtby pitted against the power of the monstrous bog holding the man in its insatiable mouth beneath the sickly green of the surface scum.

William retreated, inch by inch, as a white-knuckled Mr Holtby advanced by painfully slow degrees towards him. Neither must flounder. If both could keep their feet they could use their combined weight and energy to defeat the suction.

William felt the firm ground beneath him. Mr Holtby, he saw, had straightened up naturally and was moving his feet freely in only ankle-deep shallows. The jacket drooped loose in William's hands. They staggered a few paces up the hillside and collapsed thankfully on to the sun-baked heather.

'Thank you,' gasped Mr Holtby. 'You showed great presence of mind. I owe you an apology. I miscalculated. I try *never* to do that.'

'Featherbed Moss is a dangerous place, sir.'

'I see that. But I can beat it.'

William thought this an odd remark, and rather alarming. But Mr Holtby showed no intention of resuming the contest that day. Whatever interest he had in the bog, whether its bird life or marsh plants, seemed for the present to be satisfied.

They emptied the water out of their boots. Mr Holtby unbuttoned his gaiters. His breeches were darkly patched with wet up to his thighs. 'No matter,' he said cheerfully. 'In this sun I shall walk them dry. Not for the first time!'

He showed no desire to tramp up to the Dagger Stones or to discuss whether they had once formed a druids' circle. 'Cragdale Heights,' he said, 'and then luncheon would be a good idea.'

Amen to that, thought William.

So they walked west, skirting the treacherous fringe of the bog and striking up the steep wedge of stony ground to the craggy ramparts outlined against the sky. Clambering over that edge, they looked down again into the same valley they had left at Redford. A few miles had changed it into a picturesque dale. In front, across a mile of empty air, the hills reared up, White Horse Edge forming the next western skyline, with the Hags denting it like missing teeth.

'*Ah!*' Mr Holtby drew in his breath with deep

satisfaction. To William's relief he sat down on a convenient slab.

'Luncheon, sir?'

'By all means.'

William unpacked the basket and spread the crisp white cloth on a flat rock. With almost professional deftness he set out the guest's cutlery and plates, the folded napkin, and shining glass.

'A banquet!' cried Mr Holtby, as the cold fowl and York ham and fruit pie appeared. He declined only the bottle of red wine. 'Alas, no! When I'm working I must keep my head clear.'

Working? William snatched at the word. A clue? But it did not go far to explain Mr Holtby.

'You have some food for yourself?'

'Oh, yes, sir. Plenty. Would you like water? There's a pure spring comes straight out of the ground. Just down there. I'm going for myself . . .'

'Thank you, lad.'

William returned with two brimming tumblers of ice-cold water. Then, remembering his training, he betook himself and his lunch package to a shady corner some yards away.

Mr Holtby indeed had work to do. Before he had half finished eating he was rummaging in the leather bag, laying out notebooks and what looked like geometrical instruments. He spread out a white oblong of thick crackly paper, weighting its corners with rock fragments against the breeze. He frequently laid down his knife and fork to scribble something in his notebook. He would bend over the white paper, scowling at it intently. Twice he picked up a spy-glass and scanned the opposite side of the dale.

William's curiosity was working overtime, his imagination likewise. It was tantalizing that Mr Holtby took so long over his meal. At last William had the excuse to approach and clear up its remains.

'May I – may I ask you something, sir?'

'By all means.'

'Don't think me impertinent, sir, but could you possibly – ' He paused nervously. Father's training again.

'Yes, lad?'

'Be planning a *railway*, sir?'

2

'A shrewd question!' Mr Holtby's eyes also were shrewd, but his lips wore an approving smile.

William was relieved. He had never seen a railway. There were none within many miles of Redford and he had never been far from home. He had only read newspaper paragraphs and heard guests talking at the inn.

He could not imagine these mechanical monsters penetrating this world of rock and heather where not even a coach and horses came. Yet what else could explain Mr Holtby's odd behaviour?

He was not drawing pictures in that notebook. He seemed to be covering the pages with figures, scrawled sentences or single words, diagrams. You didn't need a protractor to compose verses. That white oblong outspread in front of him was a map.

Mr Holtby eyed him for a few moments. Then he said: 'Yes, lad. Sharp of you. A railway.'

'Really?'

'Keep it to yourself for the moment. Once rumours spread around, all kinds of trouble follow.'

'I won't breathe a word, sir!' It was thrilling to have stumbled on such an important secret.

'I shall have a word with your father tonight – I know he's a gentleman of great discretion. I wouldn't ask you to keep things from your parents. In any case the secret will soon be out. If my plan's feasible there'll have to be a bill through Parliament.'

'But – a railway up *here*, sir? Is it possible?'

'That's what I've come to find out. Fortunately my old comrades have saved me a lot of the donkey work.' He indicated the map.

'Your old comrades, sir?'

'The Royal Engineers.'

'You're a soldier, sir!'

'Not now. I grew tired of saluting men who knew far less than I did.' Mr Holtby smiled. 'I decided to become my own master. Though I still have to persuade the men with the money-bags!'

He had been in the 13th (Survey) Company of the Royal Engineers. For many years that corps had been engaged on the Ordnance Survey, gradually mapping the whole kingdom, sheet by sheet, from Kent northwards.

'By good luck,' he said, 'they reached this part of Yorkshire only a year or two ago.'

'I remember! There were soldiers up in the hills. With theodolites.' He brought out that word with some satisfaction. 'Were you with them, sir?'

'No, I'd left the service by then.'

'No one could imagine what they were doing!'

'I don't wonder. They were certainly not planning railways. The survey was started when England was expecting an invasion by Napoleon. The government thought they'd better have precise maps for defence purposes. Nelson smashed the French fleet at Trafalgar and

15

Napoleon never came after all. But the survey was a good idea in itself, so the work went on. It's still going on. And very useful I find it.' He tapped the sheet in front of him. 'The heights of all your hills are marked. The course of every river — and stream. The distances have been measured.'

The survey had been made on a scale of two inches to a mile, reduced to one inch when engraved on copper plates for printing. The delicately hachured lines indicated the steep hillsides. No wonder Mr Holtby had been so uncannily familiar with this landscape even before he set eyes on it. He could read these maps like books. He had seen this view in his mind's eye even before he set foot in Redford.

'Of course,' he explained, 'there's an infinite amount I must still check for myself. The map shows the height of the hills, not the geology beneath the surface. Can we dig tunnels? Or blast them with gunpowder? Will the roof fall in on us? Can we keep the gradients within the power of a locomotive? The new locomotives are improving all the time.'

He had lightly pencilled a line across his map, not straight, as one might have expected, but sometimes snaking with a leisurely curve.

'Trains can't go up a really steep hill,' he admitted, 'as a coach and horses can — with a tremendous struggle — for a short time. But a steam-engine doesn't *tire* as a horse does. So our motto has to be "steady does it". And remember, we don't have to get to the *top* of every hill — we can make cuttings at a lower level. Tunnels even, if we must.'

He told William of a tunnel that Mr Brunel was busy on in Wiltshire. 'It'll be two miles long, they say. Two *miles*! They're digging from both ends at the same time, Brunel's so sure they'll meet exactly. *There's* mathematics for you, my boy.'

But the Box tunnel was taking more than brilliant calculations. 'Four thousand men,' said Mr Holtby, 'three hundred horses. Working night and day. I hope we shan't have to meet costs like that.'

The line he had drawn on his own map went nowhere near Redford. It came on to the sheet at the top right-hand corner. 'No problems before that, just a straight-forward run up from the plain through the foothills. Easy country,' he said. That brought the line into the rougher uplands north of Redford. It curved between the darkly hachured slopes of Dead Man's Hill and Mad Woman's Stones, then headed straight for the gap between Dagger Stones and Lost Lass, after which it swung towards Cragdale Heights and the very spot where they were sitting.

This obviously was where the tunnels and cuttings would come in. William could not imagine any locomotive, however miraculous, puffing up to their actual picnic site.

Questions crowded to his lips. 'But, sir – '

'Yes?'

'You've drawn your line straight across Featherbed Moss! You couldn't have known then what it was like. Now you know – '

The engineer laughed. 'I certainly do. But it's much what I expected.'

'Then surely you'll have to change the line?'

17

'I may – a little. Swing more to the left, or the right, according to what we find. Featherbed may be the big challenge. But never fear. I'll find a way.' He read the doubt in William's face. 'Ever heard of Chat Moss?'

'No, sir.'

'Before your time. You'd hardly be reading newspapers ten years ago. Huge peat bog between Manchester and Liverpool. Six thousand acres or so. Yet George Stephenson built his railway slap across it. And now the businessmen of those towns can rattle backwards and forwards whenever they want to. If Stephenson could beat Chat Moss I fancy I can cope with Featherbed.'

There were several ways to tackle bog. You could do a lot by drainage. You could divert streams that fed it from the higher slopes. At the finish, though, you would probably have to build a causeway that would hold the rails and stand the weight and vibration of the train.

'In some areas you can use timber. Thousands of tree trunks, waggonloads of brushwood. Or thousands of tons of earth and rock. If we're digging a cutting and a tunnel as well there'll be ample material.'

William could see now why he was filling his notebook with calculations and scribbled observations. And why, having finished eating, he stood up and began to move about, chipping off samples of rock with a geologist's hammer. William watched keenly, careful not to distract him.

His own mind was still full of doubts. Suppose Mr Holtby brought his track across the bog, cut through the barrier of Cragdale Heights, bored his tunnel far below the ridge-line? Even though the trains emerged hundreds of feet lower than the point where he was standing, the floor of the valley still looked impossibly far beneath. The hillside fell so steeply to the river. Even a coach would have to crawl down cautiously, its rear wheels jammed with drag-shoe and skid-chain – if there was a road to drive on, which there wasn't. Such a road would have been all acute-angle bends, anyhow, which a coach and four could negotiate but (he was certain) these trains never could – they must be like strings of sausages with their long lines of trucks and carriages.

He could hardly wait to ask Mr Holtby. But the engineer was still pottering about just below him, occasionally startling a sheep from the bracken, pausing at intervals to jot down a note or stare through his spyglass at White Beacon Hags opposite.

It was so quiet up here. Voices floated up thinly from the riverside meadows. There were brisk hoofbeats from the coach-road, the barking of a farm dog. Here only the tap of Mr Holtby's little hammer, a lamb's bleat, the drone of insects. This peace was suddenly broken by a shot from the woods below.

A flock of birds fairly exploded above the treetops and went circling in panic. The echo came rolling back from the almost sheer cliffs across the dale.

No further shots followed. Probably a farmer potting a rabbit, William guessed, or a gamekeeper killing vermin. No gentlemen's shooting parties at this season. His mind went back to the problems of a railway engineer.

Soon Mr Holtby came clambering up and handed him

notebook and hammer. 'You can put those away for today.' He took off his cap and dabbed his forehead. He looked well satisfied.

'Good day's work, sir?'

'Not over yet!' Seeing William's expression he added: 'Don't worry! Over as far as you're concerned. Only the walk home. There's a path there that will lead us straight down to the coach-road and then it's easy walking to the town. But my day's work isn't ended till I've written up my notes. Midnight maybe.'

So that was why he needed a good table in his bedroom. William's new-born dream of becoming a railway engineer suffered a temporary setback.

'Tomorrow,' said his tireless companion, 'I must climb the other side. These "hags". Do you know that side of the dale?'

'Not really, sir.'

'If your father can spare you, you can carry my bag.'

'I'm sure he can, sir.' William grinned as he imitated his father's urbane ex-butler's tone. 'The convenience of our guests is our paramount concern.'

'In that case I will ask him to hire me a chaise. It can drive us to the foot of the climb and pick us up when we come down again. I've no time to waste.'

It would be another enjoyable expedition, a welcome change from being a general dogsbody at the inn.

At that moment, out of the empty world surrounding them on the ridge, an acid voice spoke.

'May I ask, sir, what you are doing on my land?'

3

Startled, they turned.

Three men stood watching them. Two were burly, clad in rough homespun and gaiters. One sandy-haired, with a double-barrelled gun slanting from the crook of his arm. The other equally tall but more heavily built, with beady eyes and a disfigured cauliflower ear. But it was clearly the third man who had spoken, insignificant in height but erect and dapper, with a self-consciously important manner. Whereas the other two were ruddy and weather-beaten, this man's sharp face was as yellow as a guinea.

William knew that face and was instantly on guard. Sir Sefton Creevey was often a central figure, elegant in his evening finery, at the annual dinners and other gatherings for which the Coach and Horses was the favourite local centre. Since buying up much of the dale below them he had earned himself the mocking nickname King of Cragdale.

Mr Holtby answered smoothly. 'I was admiring the view, sir.'

'Well you might! One of the finest in Yorkshire. I should know. It happens to be mine.'

'I beg your pardon. Should I have said "your grace"?'

'No, the Duke's land ends at the skyline, both sides of the dale. I own the valley between. My man spotted you scrambling about. Got the eye of a hawk, Gibbon has.'

The sandy-haired man with the gun smirked in self-satisfaction. His companion looked as if he had been so battered in a lifetime of bare-knuckled prize-fights that his eyes were permanently half-closed. William recognized him also. Redford people steered clear of Battling John. Since his retirement from the ring the boxer had been given a job by Sir Sefton on the estate. Sir Sefton thought his fellow magistrates were too lenient with poachers, so any caught on his land were handed over to Battling John for treatment. No one ever came back for more.

'I've a notion,' Sir Sefton went on, 'that you're this man Holtby I've been warned about.'

The engineer stiffened. 'I am Matthew Holtby, certainly.'

'And my name is Creevey. Sir Sefton Creevey. MP. I hear rumours of a madcap scheme to build a railway in these parts. And of the promoters engaging you to build it. So I was expecting you any day, sneaking about and spying out the land!'

'We call it a "preliminary survey".'

Mr Holtby remained cool and controlled. As he after-wards explained to William, sooner or later you had to come to a settlement with such people. It didn't help to build up hostility in advance.

'If that survey shows the project is feasible,' he con-tinued, 'we shall lay a private bill before Parliament – '

'I know! We have a dozen of the damned things every week. The country has gone railway mad.'

'Landowners who may be affected, like yourself –

22

indeed, anyone at all — will have a chance to raise objections — '

'And I warn you I shall!' The little man snorted. 'I shall fight your damned bill every inch of the way.' He waved his hand at the valley below. 'If you think I am going to let you ruin my property with your infernal engines — all stink, sparks and smoke — frightening the animals, scaring away the game — '

'I see very little likelihood of that.'

'How can you avoid it? There's only the one way up over the hills, the way the coach-road takes. I've built a fine house down there, overlooking the river, Cragdale Hall — '

'So I've heard, sir. One of the finest country seats in the locality,' Mr Holtby added tactfully.

'So it is. The coach-road runs past my lodge gates. Dammit, your railway would have to come just as close.'

'I'm not planning to take it through the dale at all.'

Sir Sefton gaped. 'But how else — '

'We avoid unnecessary ups and downs. Once our trains reach the necessary altitude we shall try to keep them up there until we start the gradual descent into Lancashire.'

'But Cragdale — '

'We can go *over* Cragdale.'

Sir Sefton looked dumbfounded. As Mr Holtby confidently explained, William too got the answer to the problem which had perplexed him.

A tunnel through the ridge on which they were standing would be matched by another at the same altitude in the rocky hillside facing them from White Beacon Hags.

23

Beyond that second tunnel the line should have a clear run through open moorlands into Lancashire.

'But the *gap*, man, between your two tunnels!' Sir Sefton was not convinced. 'The width! And at this height above the dale! No bridge could span it!'

'We'd need a bridge only in the middle, sir, where the line runs over the river. That central span can be approached by viaducts on both sides. Tall, slender arches, elegant — '

'*Elegant?* An eyesore!'

'No. Built of local stone from the tunnel excavations.'

'None the less, a damnable eyesore!'

'Have you travelled in France?' asked Mr Holtby mildly.

'I have travelled the world. France, naturally. As a young man I made the Grand Tour.'

'Then you have seen the Pont du Gard in Provence?'

Sir Sefton hesitated, then answered unconvincingly, 'Of course! I was shown everything worth seeing.'

'Then you'll recall the ancient Roman aqueduct spanning the valley on its line of arches?' William's own memory flew back to an engraving of it in the schoolroom. 'And you will remember,' Mr Holtby continued mercilessly, 'how universally it is still admired? Mine will be equally beautiful.'

'But hardly what one wishes to view from one's windows!'

'You'll raise this as an objection to the bill?'

'With all the eloquence at my disposal.'

'That is your privilege,' said Mr Holtby courteously.

'Some Members of Parliament may turn it to your ridicule.'

The two men were like fencers. It was as good as a play.

'What the devil do you mean, sir?' the landowner demanded.

'I haven't seen Cragdale Hall – the dot on my map does not tell me which way your windows face. But it's two miles south of here – and I doubt if it was planned to have all the principal rooms facing north. Will anyone but a servant in an attic get a glimpse of my viaducts?' Mr Holtby smiled wickedly. 'I can hear the laughter at Westminster if you brought up that argument.'

'I shan't dispute with you further,' said Sir Sefton grandly.

'You'll get appropriate compensation if the scheme goes through. I am pretty sure it will. We have the Duke on our side, a useful ally. So, I'll wish you good-day, Sir Sefton.'

He signed to William, raised his cap, and started down the hill. 'He'll come round, you'll see,' he murmured.

Far below them the Twin Roses mail coach from Lancashire was spinning smartly along. The guard sounded a warning blast so that the tollgate should be opened ready.

On that coach too there was a passenger who would be travelling no further than Redford that night, another passenger destined to influence the whole of William's future. But neither she nor William had the slightest foreknowledge of the fact.

4

She had been planning this desperate escape only for the past week, but, Caroline Callender now realized as the coach rumbled on hour by hour over the Pennine moors, the first wild hope had been born in her almost a year ago.

She thought of an earlier journey. She had been numb then, almost mindless, straight from her mother's funeral. That had followed her father's death in tragically swift succession. Stunned by the second loss she had let herself be gathered up like a parcel by her uncle and aunt, and bundled into the coach for that endless journey to Lancashire.

She remembered their voices, strangers' voices then, afterwards all too familiar. Uncle Daniel's, masterful as always: 'Of *course* you must come back with us to Eldonby! Where else can you go? You can't stay in York!' And Aunt Louisa's, plaintive, with her apologetic little stammer: 'I'm your poor mother's only sister! It's my *duty*.' Uncle Daniel had weighed in again: 'How could we leave you in that fever-ridden slum? What would people *say*?'

Over the next few weeks sensation had gradually returned. She began to live again. Uncle Daniel's house seemed huge. Magnificent. Screened off by massed foliage from the mean streets and the cotton-mills from which his wealth came. There were so many rooms, over-large, over-furnished, over-decorated, absurd for so small a family; her uncle and aunt had only the one child, her cousin Bob, and he was out all day at the mill, learning how to take his share in the management. Most of the time the spacious rooms were silent and empty except for the servants dusting and polishing – and the stately patrolling of Aunt Louisa's cats on their noiseless feet.

If only there had been a dog, just one dog, to bring vitality to the place! But her aunt had a horror of dogs, and in this Uncle Daniel humoured her, banning dogs of any sort on the premises. That was no great self-denial for him. He cared for no four-footed creature, whether horse or hedgehog.

It was all very different from the slum vicarage in York where her father had felt called to work among the poor.

Being human, Caroline had to admit to enjoying the comfort and luxury. Food that would never have found its way to her parents' economical table. Clothes that Aunt Louisa insisted on buying her, promising that 'once you are out of mourning' there would be no limit to the expensive finery that would be hers. Caroline tried to express her gratitude. Her aunt, she realized, had a heart of gold fluttering inside her insipid exterior. Usually Uncle Daniel would answer smugly on her behalf.

'We want you to have the best of everything, child. God in His wisdom has taken away your father and mother – but in His infinite goodness He has given you us to replace them.'

'Yes, uncle,' she said. The words almost choked her.

27

Her cousin, even when at home, was a disappointment. It was Bob's fate to be a disappointment. Above all, to his own father. 'I should ha' sent him away to college,' Uncle Daniel growled on one occasion. 'Given him a bit o' polish. Then, wi' my brass behind him, he could have mixed wi' anybody.'

Caroline had hoped for some human contact at least with a boy only three years older than herself. But even with her Bob showed no disposition to mix. Was he really so uncouth or just shy? Or just worn out by a long day in the mill? He was certainly crushed by his father's personality.

Once she tried to draw him out by asking questions relating to his work. He came to life somewhat then. She could tell that he had ambitions. He became almost animated when explaining some improvement in the machinery. She could not follow him there, preferring to hear about the work people he dealt with.

'I should like to see the mill,' she said.

He was horrified. 'I couldn't possibly take you round. A young girl like you!'

'But you said there were girls of seven or eight – only half my age! Working there from morn till night! I've heard there are people called "strappers".' She challenged him. 'What exactly is a "strapper"?'

'Sometimes the girls doze off at their work,' he said sulkily.

'I don't wonder, with such long hours.'

'You don't realize – it's vital they keep awake at the looms. The cloth can be ruined, the whole production of the mill depends . . . so they must have a flick of the strap

28

if we notice their eyes closing.' He read the indignation in her face. He tried to soothe her. 'They're used to it,' he said.

'How can their *parents* — '

'Their parents are keen enough to get them into the mills. They need the money to keep the family alive. We don't have many jobs for the grown men. The mothers come, but they're for ever breaking off to have babies. And most of the women drop out anyhow in their thirties or forties.'

'Worn out, I should imagine!'

'Maybe. It's the way things are. Even if we could run our mills without child labour the folk themselves could never manage. They'd starve. Do you know what the best hand-loom weaver takes home at the end of a week?'

'I've no idea.'

'Then you shouldn't try to argue about things you don't understand. Five shillings. If he's lucky. A man can't raise a family on that.'

She had no answer. So this was how men like Uncle Daniel built up their fortunes.

Uncle Daniel also owned a local coalmine. Bob had little first-hand knowledge of that, but one of the younger maids, Emily, who had been assigned to Caroline for little personal services and had quickly become the nearest thing to a friend that she had found in Eldonby, did. Outwardly Emily was demure and discreet, but when they were alone together she was outspoken. She had an uncle in the mine. Compared with conditions underground, existence in the mills was easy.

'The coal-owners want all the children they can get,'

29

said Emily. 'Smaller the better. Common sense! Some of those passages are only eighteen inches high.'

'Eighteen *inches*?' Caroline cried out in horror. She held up her hands instinctively, measuring the distance, familiar from her own attempts at dressmaking.

'No more, miss,' said Emily grimly.

The men at the coal-face loaded the trucks, which were hauled away by boys and girls crawling on hands and knees with a chain passing back between their legs. Stripped to the waist, the girls too.

'Shameful!' said Caroline.

'Modesty's not much on their minds, I should think! It's nearly pitch black down there, any road.'

There were ventilation doors at intervals, which had to be opened and shut to let the trucks through. These were handled by even smaller children, the 'trappers', not strong enough yet to haul the coal. They crouched alone in a tiny space, sometimes for up to sixteen hours. When children grew too big to haul trucks along the passages they could stay on and work the pumps that stopped the mine from flooding.

'It's really heavy work, that,' said Emily. 'Almost without a pause, and over their ankles in water. *Their* day is only twelve hours.' She pronounced the word 'only' with deep sarcasm. Her parents had spared no effort to save their children from such a fate. Emily had helped them in the tiny shop they kept until she attained her highest possible objective, service with a good family.

These conversations fed Caroline's determination to escape somehow – she could not yet imagine how – from this house where she would never be happy. She began to see more and more clearly the foundations on which Uncle Daniel's fortune rested. This was how the luxury and splendour were paid for. She could guess what her father would have felt about it. It was not just the distance between Eldonby and York that had made for the lack of contact between her mother and Aunt Louisa.

Uncle Daniel boasted that he was a self-made man. His shrewdness and aggressive personality had made him successful in the cotton trade. Now that he had acquired the local coal-pit more profits were flowing in. Caroline guessed that, smug though he seemed, he was beginning to wonder if money was everything.

He was developing into a snob. She, born and bred in a cathedral city, knew all about snobbery – and hated it. As a parson's daughter, even a poor parson, she was a step above some of the girls she would have loved to have as friends. Clergymen had their own grades. Her father, trudging through his parish alleyways, was a nobody compared with a canon at the Minster. The Dean was a little god. Eldonby had similar distinctions. Uncle Daniel looked down on shopkeepers and his work people were no more than the ground underfoot. But in spite of all his efforts he could not break into the charmed circle of the local gentry.

This irked him intensely. 'Dammit,' she heard him burst out to Aunt Louisa, 'I could buy most of 'em up tomorrow!'

Aunt Louisa had no ambitions for herself but rejoiced when her husband got any of the recognition he wanted.

One morning she was positively fluttering with delight. 'Your uncle is to be a *magistrate*! With JP after his name! "Justice of the Peace",' she added, in case Caroline did not fully appreciate the honour. 'He'll mix with all the other gentlemen on the bench. They can't cold-shoulder him now.'

Caroline soon realized, with alarm, that she herself might be involved in her uncle's ambitious schemes.

In York she had been to a little private school which took clergymen's daughters at reduced fees. In Eldonby he insisted that she should complete her education at Miss Davenham's Academy for Young Ladies. She seized on the opportunity gratefully. She was determined to be independent as soon as possible. She would have scrubbed floors to earn her own living, but in practice almost the only work open to a girl like herself was that of a governess or assistant teacher. She needed another year or two at school, and testimonials to her ability and character, before she could say thank-you to her aunt and uncle and march out into the freedom of the world.

On the first day she discovered that she had been enrolled as Caroline Snaith. 'But, Miss Davenham! My name is Callender!'

'I know, Caroline. I'm well aware of your sad circumstances. But your uncle wished to enter you under his own name.'

'But – ' Caroline's face flamed with outrage. '*I* wasn't asked. Mr Snaith is not my father.'

Miss Davenham pursed her lips. She was not used to arguments. 'No one will pretend he is. But it is simpler. It will save you constant explanations.'

Caroline consoled herself, when she had calmed down, that nobody would imagine that she was Uncle Daniel's daughter. Eldonby was a town in which everybody knew everybody else. Uncle Daniel had lived there all his life and it was common knowledge that Bob was his only child. She was resentful at being entered in the school register under his name, but she *was* his niece. Uncles and nieces could just as easily have the same surname. And he *was* paying her fees. It was not worth a row which would have upset Aunt Louisa.

It was only several months later that she saw why he was so interested in her getting a good education. She had taken her school books up to her bedroom. Sitting on the cushioned windowseat, the window wide open to the scents of the garden, she overheard her uncle and aunt talking on the terrace below.

'She's getting so *pretty*.' Aunt Louisa's quaver was unusually emphatic.

'Pretty? The girl's going to be an absolute stunner.' It was equally rare for him to be so flattering.

Caroline knew she ought to move away from the window, but she was too human to do so. She must know if they were talking about her.

They were. 'My sister had hair like that. The colour of honey, people used to say. How I envied her!'

'Well, they'll soon be buzzing round her like bees.' It was not in her uncle's nature to keep his voice down. 'Mark my words,' he went on, 'we'll be talking of marriage in a year or two.'

Aunt Louisa sounded incredulous, alarmed yet gratified. 'But – but we know so few people! Of the right sort.'

'We know nobody of the right sort,' he said harshly.

'The Simpsons have those three boys – '

'Another family in cotton,' he said contemptuously. 'That kind of marriage will have to do for Bob. He'll get no higher. Even with my brass behind him. Caroline's a very different kettle of fish.'

Caroline was not best pleased with the phrase, but he clearly meant it as a compliment. Cautiously she poked her head out of the window a little further, not to miss a word as Uncle Daniel unfolded his grand design.

With her looks the girl would attract notice as soon as she left Miss Davenham's, put her hair up, and was seen at local functions. Coming from York she would bring a slight aura of gentility to this town of clogs and cobbles. As niece of Daniel Snaith Esquire, JP – or by then, better still, as his adopted daughter – she would make an attractive bride for the son of some less prosperous landed gentleman.

'And there's no lack o' them just now,' he assured Aunt Louisa, 'what wi' the run o' bad harvests and now they may be going to abolish the Corn Laws. They know a daughter o' Daniel Snaith's would bring a sizeable dowry to any marriage arranged for her.'

Listening, Caroline was first fascinated, then nauseated, by what he was planning. She told herself it was just his daydream, designed to impress Aunt Louisa. But over the next few months things cropped up, casual remarks and indications, which she saw as essential pieces to be fitted into his programme.

She was learning how his mind worked. Once, at the

dinner-table, he was holding forth to Bob how some devious business transaction should be managed. There were times to trick your rival into a merger and then to swallow him. Times to fight him openly and ruthlessly until he went bankrupt. 'If you're climbing a cliff,' he said, 'you must decide when to go straight up and when to move sideways. All what matters is getting to the top.' She knew now that he did not confine that approach to commercial deals.

One evening Aunt Louisa murmured: 'Your uncle and I were wondering, my dear – how you would feel – we should like to adopt you as our daughter?' So the plan was moving on. It was like ticking off dates on a calendar.

'It's just a notion we had,' said Uncle Daniel hastily, more gently than usual. 'No need to decide anything now.'

'I – I'll think about it,' she forced herself to say. 'You're very kind.'

She had decided in that instant. She must – somehow – escape.

5

Escape. But where? To whom?

The questions kept her awake far into the night.

She had no other close relative, no one with more claim on her than Aunt Louisa. That in practice meant Uncle Daniel. Who would risk a legal battle with him?

She could think of people in York who might have helped her in any other sort of difficulty. In this case they would be powerless. They were not relations, they had no standing. Anyhow, she dared not go to York. It was the first place he would look for her – and drag her back to Lancashire.

She remembered childhood stories in which the ill-treated heroine ran away from home, had alarming adventures in sinister forests and gruesome castles, but could depend on a blissful ending by the last page. Real life, she knew, was different.

In a slum parish you learnt early about real life, especially if your parents were known as compassionate people. You overheard much, you picked up more than you were supposed to know. You knew what more often happened when girls ran away. You met them on the vicarage doorstep, girls with black eyes or worse injuries, girls with babies wrapped in their shawls, girls with both.

Whatever Caroline's despair she would not run away

until she had a clear idea of where she was going.

If only she could share her problem . . . It would be unfair to confide in Emily. It would cost the maid her job if she knew Caroline's plans but did not give them away. Caroline had made no close school-friend at Miss Davenham's Academy. The other girls had all grown up together in Eldonby. They had long ago woven their web of best-friend alliances and, as a newly arrived outsider from Yorkshire, she'd not been admitted to their close relationships. She alone had no 'best friend'.

Unlike her mother, when *she* was a girl. She had had a really devoted friend. She and her Matty might have been sentimental, vowing eternal loyalty to each other, but the relationship had lasted. Matty had gone into service, moved out of the district, but kept in touch. In due course they had both married, had children, felt deeper emotions, acquired more demanding loyalties. Despite all that, despite distances which made meetings impossible, the bond had remained. 'If anything ever happened to your dear father – God forbid!' said her mother, 'Matty's still the first person I'd turn to.' Caroline wished now that she had a friend like that.

Then, instantly, the thought flashed into her mind: but I *have!* She remembered how her mother's face would light up when she unfolded the annual Christmas letter. 'She sends you her good wishes – she always asks after you!' 'But she's never set eyes on me – ' 'But you're *my* daughter!'

Probably this Mrs Thornton had never been told of her friend's death. Where was it she lived? Her husband kept an inn. A town in Yorkshire. Redford. The mail coach ran there across the hills from Eldonby. It was called the Twin Roses because it linked the two counties. Her mother's words came back to her: 'Matty's the first person I'd turn to.'

Uncle Daniel would never think of Redford. The town clock was striking midnight. After much excited thinking sleep came. Next morning she continued more calmly to face realities.

What would she say if this woman she had never seen told her she must turn round and go straight back to Eldonby? Or, though sympathetic enough, could not offer her shelter? I am not coming back here, Caroline vowed. After my coach fare I shall have two pounds. I can find cheap lodgings. I shall look for work.

She was still too young to become a governess. She had no experience of employment, no testimonials to honesty – but this Matty would surely speak for her. She would find some work, however rough or dirty. She would *not* live under her uncle's roof and answer to a name that was not hers. 'Miss Snaith', indeed! She would not provide a step for Uncle Daniel's climb into genteel society. I shall trust in the Lord, she decided firmly. She had been told to often enough.

The local newspaper showed that the Twin Roses Flyer left the Lamb and Flag at half-past six every Monday, Wednesday and Friday morning. The fare was a pound, half price if one braved the weather and rode on top. That was really for gentlemen. A girl clambering up to an outside seat would be conspicuous. That was the last thing she could afford to be. Her method of leaving the town must remain a secret.

A young lady travelling alone at that early hour would be remembered anyhow. Within a few hours her uncle would know where she was heading for – he might even hire a fast chaise and overtake her.

She must go back to an idea she had already considered and rejected because it had been so overworked in romantic stories, even Shakespeare's plays. Runaway heroines dressed up as boys, fooling everyone in a most improbable manner. She had dismissed it as ridiculous. Now she wondered if, after all, it *was* so ridiculous. Who, in the early morning bustle, would take a second glance at an unknown youth, especially if he had bought his ticket the previous day?

Even the disguise was no problem. A few days ago she had been helping her aunt in one of the charitable efforts which provided an outlet for her suppressed personality. They had been sorting discarded clothes in an attic, to distribute to the poor.

'This was Bob's.' Aunt Louisa held up a coat. 'Plenty of wear in it. He's grown so fast, he'll never get into it again.'

'Or these trousers!' Caroline laughed.

'And he looked *so* elegant.' Her aunt sounded wistful. She hesitated as if embarrassed. 'Only, my dear – '

'Yes, aunt?'

'A young lady really should not speak of "trousers". It is more proper to refer to the garments as "unmentionables".'

'I'll remember,' Caroline promised demurely.

39

The sorted cast-offs still lay waiting for distribution. Her own slender legs – 'sorry, aunt,' she corrected herself silently, 'my nether limbs' – would surely fit into even those tightly tailored unmentionables. She had the figure for the disguise. At the York school she had been the natural choice for Viola in the scenes from *Twelfth Night*.

Walking home from Miss Davenham's on the following Tuesday, her plans by then perfected, she slipped into the coaching office at the Lamb and Flag.

'My brother wants a seat on the Twin Roses Flyer tomorrow. An outside seat, please. He was most particular.'

The bleary-eyed old man peered at the bookings. 'Then he's just lucky, miss. One left. Ten shillings.' She laid down the coins. 'And the name, please?'

She was prepared for that. 'Jennings,' she said.

'Warn him to come in good time. Coach won't wait.'

She doubted if the old man would retain much memory of her if questioned. She would not figure in the written record, only the invented young Jennings. She went off, elated. It would have been maddening to wait two more days.

The hardest thing now was the letter to poor Aunt Louisa. She must not hurt her feelings. Caroline had nothing against her, she had meant well – and she was her mother's sister. After much chewing of the pen Caroline wrote:

'*You must not think me ungrateful for your kind generosity, but I feel I can no longer accept it. I am sure I can make my own way in the world and that it is my duty to try.*' 'Duty' seemed the right word to use in a letter her uncle was certain to read.

'*I appreciate Uncle's offer to adopt me, but I owe it to my dear Father's memory to remain Caroline Callender.*'

Best to keep the letter short. The adoption plan had been only the last straw, but to list all her other reasons would only have caused her aunt pain. She went on: '*Please do not worry about me. I am going to friends.*' She hoped fervently that this would prove true. '*When I am more permanently settled I will write again.*' She ended with apologies for any distress caused and signed herself emphatically '*Caroline Callender*'.

She hoped it would not sound heartlessly cool, but she must give no clues. No reference to long journeys or Yorkshire, no apology for taking Bob's cast-offs. It could be weeks before her aunt noticed their disappearance, by which time it would not matter.

That evening she took her candle and went up to bed in good time. Her visit to the attics was accomplished without meeting any of the servants. Back in her own room with her disguise, she was seized by a fear that those narrow nankeen trousers might not fit. Alarmed, she slipped off her dress and petticoat, hoping to keep on her ankle-length pantalettes. It was quite a struggle to force her legs down the tapering unmentionables – it meant crushing the lacy frills of the pantalettes – but she managed it. She pulled the trousers up to her waist and buttoned the flap in front. Yes, they fitted, so neatly indeed that they would have stayed up without the broad tapes crossing her shoulders. She could fasten the straps that passed under her shoes.

The coat was not too tight or the buttoned-up waistcoat, which, with a very full cravat beneath her chin, would completely conceal her lack of a boy's shirt beneath.

Luckily she had just stripped off her disguise when – most unusually – there was a diffident tap on the door and her aunt's whisper: 'You are not asleep, Caroline?'

'No, aunt – '

Hastily she flung her discarded dress and petticoat over the tell-tale garments on the bed. Aunt Louisa came in, candlestick in hand.

'I – I feared you were not quite yourself this evening. That you were indisposed – '

'Oh, no, I'm perfectly well. Quite myself.' Never *more* myself, thought Caroline.

'I often wish we could talk more together. I hope if ever . . .' Aunt Louisa's voice tailed away ineffectually.

Caroline felt guilty. She *ought* to have talked to her aunt before making this decision. But what use would it have been? Uncle Daniel would have overwhelmed his wife. If her own resolution had wavered at that moment it would have been stiffened by Aunt Louisa's next remark.

'Your uncle and I are so fond of you, my dear. He has great plans for you.'

Caroline knew what plans. 'I'm sure he has.' She was more determined than ever not to fall in with them.

Aunt Louisa clucked at the untidy room. 'I'll help you to hang up your clothes.'

'No, really, aunt. You do too much for me.' She tried to conceal her panic with a light tone. 'I'm growing up, I'm not a child, I must learn to look after myself.' She thrust her aunt's candlestick back into her hand and steered her gently back to the door. 'But thank you – thank you for everything.' She gave Aunt Louisa an affectionate good-night kiss and was thankful afterwards she had seized the opportunity.

She must pack. She would have liked to take not a stitch that her uncle had paid for, but she had brought so little from York. She would need girl's clothes again as soon as she was clear away. She had two dresses she could not bear to leave behind. She would need petticoats, a change of underclothes besides the chemisette and pantalettes she would be wearing, stockings, shoes, slippers . . . Room must somehow be found in the bag for them all.

Her other possessions were few. The little watch, her parents' last birthday present, she would slip into her waistcoat pocket. Their miniature portraits would take up little space, but she could not carry her beloved books, except the well-thumbed copy of *Pride and Prejudice* inscribed from Papa. She squeezed it between the folds of clothing in the bag. Her mother's rings were in Aunt Louisa's safe keeping – she would not have taken them anyhow, in case of loss or theft or the dreadful temptation to sell them in case of need. Common sense told her that this secret flight would not make a permanent break with her aunt. Anything she could not take with her now could be sent for at some later date.

Her one dread was of missing the coach. She must be out of the house before the servants got up. Dared she get into bed and risk oversleeping? To be safe she settled herself in a low chair, comfortable but not dangerously so. Somehow she got through the night, with short snatches of uneasy sleep broken by the striking of the town clock or the horn of a coach. When she woke at four the candle had burnt down but the gathering greyness of the room allowed her to read the time on her watch. The window was soon a pink oblong of midsummer dawn.

Thankfully she gave up all pretence of resting. She jumped up, splashed her face and arms with cold water from the jug, and, having studied her hair in the mirror, attacked it reluctantly with her scissors. It must be done. How lucky, though, she had not done it before Aunt Louisa's visit! She would not sacrifice more than she was compelled. Many young gentlemen were growing their hair long, like Mr Disraeli with his black curls in the House of Commons. She must be careful to gather up all the clippings from the bedroom floor, stuff them into a stocking, and take them away with her, or they would betray the fact that she'd gone in male disguise.

Her watch warned her she should be off before the house began to stir. She finished her preparations, glanced round to check that she had forgotten nothing, propped the note for her aunt on the mantelpiece, opened the door stealthily, and tiptoed down the main staircase. From the drawing-room she passed through to the orangery, and thence, unbolting the door to the gardens, out on to the terrace. A shrubbery gave cover as far as the orchard. She would not be seen even by a yawning kitchen-maid at an attic window. One more bolt to slide back, the wooden gate set in the high orchard wall. She found herself on the canal towing-path.

A favourite place for strollers — she liked it herself — but it should be deserted at this hour. It was, except for a man leading the massive horse which towed his barge. 'Top o' the mornin', lad!' he called cheerfully, and she remembered in time not to drop her eyes but to smile back with a boy's jauntiness. She would have assumed the swagger she had put on for *Twelfth Night* but who could swagger when carrying such a heavy bag?

She had time to kill, now that she was safely clear of the house. She must not hang about at the inn, conspicuous, waiting for the coach to start. She was suddenly aware that the nervous strains of the night had left her ravenously hungry. She walked a little distance beside the still green water of the canal, then sat down under a hawthorn, and unwrapped the food she had managed to smuggle up to her room. Bread, cold ham, a wedge of fruit cake. Then she picked up her bag again and walked on at a leisurely pace.

She met no one else till she turned off the path into the streets. The millworkers had been at their looms long ago, but the town was just waking to life, shutters coming down, windows opening, carts rumbling. Nowhere was livelier than the yard of the Lamb and Flag.

The coach stood ready, washed and polished, its black and maroon sides glistening in the sun. The horses were being backed into position and harnessed. A lady and gentleman stood waiting to climb in when given the word. Two more couples drove up in private carriages as she arrived, greeting each other with polite murmurs. A cluster of top-hatted men stood laughing and joking.

A tall guard, also in a top hat with a curly brim, rather imposing in his long braided coat, was checking each passenger and depositing his luggage with the mail bags

45

in the spacious boot. He took Caroline's bag and stowed it with the others. 'Mr Jennings?'

'Yes.'

'You're a fortunate young man.'

'Fortunate?'

'You get the box-seat next the driver. These gentlemen want to keep together, so they'll all sit behind with me. You'll have Waterloo Walter to yourself. An honour that many a gentleman would pay an extra guinea for.'

'I'm lucky then,' she said and meant it. She would enjoy the privileged seat for its own sake, but also it would be easier to keep up the pretence with one man, intent on his driving, than with that jovial, chattering group behind.

The driver had appeared and was running a critical eye over his team. He seemed to know each horse by name and disposition. The guard glanced at the official coach clock behind its glass panel, where even he could not tamper with it. 'Time to be off, then. All aboard, gentlemen, *if* you please!'

From habit Caroline hesitated. She was used to a helping hand. Idiot, she thought angrily. Who would offer a helping hand to a boy in his teens? She grasped the brass rail and climbed – neatly, she hoped – to the seat beside the driver.

Waterloo Walter was staring straight ahead of him, the long reins firmly between his fingers. The guard blew a warning blast for incautious passers-by in the street outside. The horses came to life, wheeled majestically under the arch, and broke into their disciplined trot. At last, she thought, with a great lightening of the heart, they were off. The town fell behind them. In front rose the long green line of the Pennine fells.

6

'Grand day.' The coachman spoke for the first time.

She had felt too shy to speak first. He was an impressive figure in his long coat with its extra layers of thick cloth to protect his shoulders from the cruellest weather. She marvelled at his control of those four powerful horses with their reins bunched in his left hand.

What should she call him? You could not call a coachman 'sir', however important he looked. With a day in front of them she must call him something. 'May I know your name?' she asked politely. 'I heard the gentlemen call you "Waterloo" – is that really – '

He turned and grinned down at her. 'Ay, lad, they call me "Waterloo Walter". But *you* won't,' he added firmly. 'To you I'm "Mester Armstrong". But very much at your service.'

'Were you at the battle?' Wellington's defeat of Napoleon was a legend that had dominated her childhood.

He chuckled. 'I've a medal to prove it.'

'You'd be in the cavalry?' It was a reasonable guess for a man with such mastery of horses. Perhaps a Life Guard or a dragoon.

'Nay, lad, a gunner. In the Horse Artillery. That's where I learnt to handle a team. They took some handling, too, in the middle of a battle.'

She supposed that a gunner would be in less danger than other soldiers. She pictured the cannon lining some ridge in the rear, firing over the heads of troops in front. She supposed wrong.

'The Duke had the infantry formed up in squares, shoulder to shoulder, so solid even Boney's cavalry couldn't break through their bayonets. We couldn't fire our guns from inside a square. We had to gallop up into the open spaces between, unlimber, pepper the French soon as they were near enough – '

She gasped. It sounded risky. Waterloo Walter was gratified.

'Very last moment we had to bolt like mad and slip inside the nearest square. We took a wheel off each gun, so they couldn't take 'em away. Soon as they'd gone we had to nip out, fit the wheel on again, and load ready for the next charge.'

'It must have been awful. You had to run for your lives.'

'If we didn't,' he said grimly, 'we didn't have a second chance. Those sabres would swish your arm off – or your head – quick as that. The lancers would spit you like a partridge.'

A boy, no doubt, would have enjoyed this bloodcurdling recital. Waterloo would suppose that she did. To discourage him she said: 'I think war is frightful.'

'So it is, lad. I can't ever forget those horses,' he said soberly. 'We men were there from choice, more fools us. Those poor beasts were innocent.' Her opinion of him warmed.

Behind them Gentleman Joe, the guard, sounded a

warning toot. They were nearing the next stage. How quickly, she thought, this first hour had gone by.

Never before had she realized the extraordinary efficiency of the royal mail. Only a few minutes were allowed for the halt. In that space not only had the team to be changed but Gentleman Joe had to unlock the boot, hand out the local mail bags and accept others, check any fresh passengers joining the coach, and, most vital of all, get his time-bill signed by the postmaster. If the coach was running late the postmaster must record the fact and the reason.

'Joe has to report *me* if I break any rules,' said Waterloo, 'and contrariwise I'm expected to report *him*.'

'Do you ever?'

He laughed. 'When you work together you learn to live and let live.'

On the empty moorland roads conversation was easy. He talked about his work and was obviously flattered by her interest.

The stages were about ten miles apart, an hour's run at trotting speed. Here stages were sometimes closer, because of the punishing gradients. There were eight stages on the Twin Roses route.

'So you drive thirty-two different horses in the day?'

'Ay. And you can't bank on the same ones each time.'

'Can you tell one from another?'

He smiled. 'You soon learn. Johnny there – the left-hand leader. Good beast, but a miller.'

'A miller?'

'Kicks.'

He let her into the mysteries of coachman's language.

A 'lame hand' was a bad driver, liable to 'feather-edge it' by trying to take a sharp corner too close. The horses were the 'cattle', a coach was a 'drag', a whip a 'tool'. He himself seldom used one; he could control his team with the 'ribbons', each rein attached to an individual animal, leader or wheeler, left or right. The ribbons ran between fingers and thumb, as carefully arranged as a hand of cards.

The landscape grew wilder, the hamlets smaller. He pointed out trouble-spots, high-arched bridges where the road got flooded, a bank where you might be blocked by a landslide, stretches where the snow drifted badly.

'That's where Gentleman Joe has to get his shovel out.'

They must be ready for anything, from a fallen horse to a serious breakdown. The tool-kit included hatchet and hammer, saw and wrench, spare chains, nails, screws, rope, everything. In a breakdown Joe's first duty was to the mails. He must unharness a horse and ride it to the next stage with the bags, If the snowdrifts were too deep, he must somehow struggle through with them on foot.

'And are you ever stopped by highwaymen?'

'Nay, that was more in the old days.' But the mail must be protected. Regulations required every guard to carry a blunderbuss, a brace of pistols, powder-horn and ammunition, the weapons loaded at all times.

She dared not ask if the two men were adequately paid for these heroic duties. Later she was shocked to learn that coachmen earned only a pound a week and guards half as much. But most of them could reckon on several more pounds a week from the tips they were not supposed to accept.

The sun was now beating down from a cloudless sky.

51

Waterloo seemed untroubled by the heat. He would no more have removed that layered coat than a guardsman would have stripped off his scarlet tunic. Caroline was thankful that at least her borrowed trousers were of thin nankeen, the lightweight buff cotton material which Uncle Daniel's mill, like so many in Lancashire, had copied from the Chinese.

At midday they pulled up at the lonely moorland inn which marked the fourth stage. The guard sang out the eagerly awaited announcement:

'Dinner-time stop! They'll have good food ready on the table. Twenty minutes only!'

A welcoming landlady in the doorway led the three women discreetly aside. Unthinkingly Caroline began to follow, but their guide swung round and barred the way. 'No, sir,' she positively hissed. 'Over yonder — across the yard!'

Crestfallen, Caroline headed for the archway indicated, only to find that all the gentlemen had preceded her. Mercifully they had their backs to her and were concentrating their gaze upon a blank wall. To her relief she spied a small half-open door in the far corner. She hurried to it with averted eyes and flaming cheeks.

When she emerged again the men had vanished to the coffee-room, where they could be heard clamouring for drinks. She followed and squeezed into a vacant seat. A savoury plateful of food appeared in front of her and she attacked it with enthusiasm.

On the next stage, as they drove over a crest, Joe surprised them all with a few bars of 'Ilkley Moor' on the key-bugle which he preferred, as many guards did, to the traditional long horn on which they could not play tunes. He had already that morning entertained them with snatches of favourite country airs, dances and even scraps of Mozart.

'We've crossed into Yorkshire now,' Waterloo explained. Her heart leapt.

He began to talk of cricket. She replied cagily. It seemed safe to agree warmly with whatever he said. She had once watched the Minster choristers engaged in that mysterious game, but was still no wiser. She was thankful when they stopped again to change horses and could change the subject too.

When they drove on again, across the rolling wastes of heather, he said: 'I hear talk – we pick up all sorts of rumour on the road – about some wild scheme to build a railway up here.'

'How on earth – ' she exclaimed incredulously.

'You may well ask, lad.'

He had nothing against the new-fangled invention. It was very well, in flat country, for shifting coal and bricks and suchlike weighty loads. Quicker than canals. 'But for people – ' He snorted. 'A gentleman will always choose to drive behind real horses, not iron ones.'

What luck, she thought, getting this seat beside such a coachman! His flow of conversation took her mind off the anxieties of this day. She had little chance to worry how she would be received at the end of the journey. And if she had been sitting with the other passengers it would have been a constant effort to keep up her deception and parry their inquisitive questions.

They were descending now into a deep dale. Twice Joe had to jump down and fix the iron shoe to one of the back wheels to brake its progress. The shaggy moors gave place to green hillsides patterned with pale drystone walls. Cattle grazed as well as sheep. Once the guard mischievously raised his bugle and imitated the mooing of a cow so convincingly that a dozen beasts came thundering down the field to stare in puzzlement at the passing coach.

'A real musician, Joe,' said Waterloo admiringly. And all the passengers applauded his skill.

They were bowling along a well-made road under noble trees, crossing and recrossing a river that foamed round moss-grown boulders. The coachman waved his free hand at two figures coming down from the heights above. 'My young friend William,' he explained. 'A decent lad. You'd like William. Don't know the man.' Coachman and guard slept every other night at the Yorkshire end of the run, so they had a nodding acquaintance with some of the Redford people.

Two miles further on he pointed out a mansion standing back from the road. 'Cragdale House. Sir Sefton Creevey built it only ten years ago – for all the Gothic towers and battlements. Must ha' cost a pretty penny.'

But expense, it seemed, had been no object. Sir Sefton had been a great plantation owner in Jamaica. He'd owned thousands of acres of sugarcane and slaves to work them. He'd looked ahead and reckoned that slavery wouldn't last for ever. So – being a crafty devil, said Waterloo, he'd sold out while the going was good, and brought his fortune back to England. 'Trouble is, he expects everyone here to bow down to him as they had to do in the West Indies. Folks hereabouts make fun of him, call him the "King of Cragdale". He thinks his money can buy everything.'

'I've known people like that,' said Caroline darkly.

They were nearing Redford. The grey stone houses rose in front. Gentleman Joe sounded his horn, Waterloo Walter took his team through the open tollgates at a spanking pace. Far down the High Street she saw the inn-sign, end of the journey and start of the next chapter in her adventure. She braced herself for what would happen in the next few minutes.

First though there was another ordeal, trivial but daunting all the same — to tip this magnificent coachman and with nothing more lavish than a shilling. The coach came to a standstill in the yard. She groped in her pocket and moistened her lips, she jumped down and turned, holding out the humble coin. 'I'd like to thank you, Mr Armstrong, for a most interesting journey.'

He smiled down at her. 'Nay, keep it. Been most interestin' for me too. Go careful – an' best o' luck – lass!'

The last word was murmured. Her jaw dropped. 'You *guessed*?'

He dropped down beside her. 'Had my suspicions early on. Tested 'em by talking o' cricket. You agreed with all I said – utter nonsense though it was! Knew then I was right. Don't worry.' He laid a finger across his lips. 'I'll not blab.'

She almost reached up and kissed him. But that would

55

have given the secret away to everyone. She could only give him a special smile. She turned and claimed her bag from Gentleman Joe, who accepted her shilling respectfully.

She walked into the inn and caught the eye of a maid. 'Where can I find Mrs Thornton?'

'That was her, sir, just gone up the stairs.'

'I must see her — an urgent message — ' Before the maid could stop her Caroline dived in pursuit.

Mrs Thornton heard the hurrying footsteps behind her and paused with her hand on the knob of the door she was about to open. 'Who are you? What are you doing up here?' She was a brisk little woman, businesslike but kindly.

'I — I'm sorry. I — I think you were my mother's friend. Mrs Callender. At York.'

The bright little face softened. 'Emma Callender?' she cried. Her expression changed again. 'But Emma never *had* a boy,' she said suspiciously.

'No. I'm Caroline.'

Mrs Thornton stood the shock well. 'Of *course*! Caroline! I remember. I see the likeness. The hair — but what *have* you done to it? You'd better come in here.'

They entered what looked like her private sitting-room. There was a tea-tray on the table. Mrs Thornton produced another cup and saucer. She pushed aside some household accounts.

Caroline told her story. What a relief it was to have such a sympathetic listener! 'You poor child,' said Mrs Thornton when she paused for breath. 'Your mother was never happy about Louisa's marriage. *I* never liked the sound of that Daniel Snaith. You did right to come to me.'

'I didn't know where to turn to.' Never one for easy tears Caroline suddenly found herself fighting them.

'I must talk to my husband – we must decide what's best. You have some of your own clothes in this bag?'

'Oh, yes.'

'Then you must change at once. You're just off the coach? No one's seen you but the maid?'

'And only for a moment!'

'She'll not remember. There's such a flurry when a coach comes in. Get out of these clothes – from that moment the wicked young lad will cease to exist and a blameless young lady will be born. But you must take off these things now.'

Willingly Caroline opened her bag and spread out her normal garments. Off came the cravat, the coat and waistcoat. The nankeen unmentionables fell crumpled around her ankles. She was struggling with them, having forgotten to unbuckle the straps that passed beneath her shoes, when the door was flung open.

'*William!*'

Mrs Thornton's voice was that of a woman who could control a busy inn as effectively as Waterloo Walter could control an unruly team. 'Wait outside,' she commanded, 'until I call you in!'

7

William backed out with a choked apology. His instinct was to come back later. But he had been told to wait outside, so he did so. Who was the unknown apparition?

Very soon his mother opened the door and called him in. A girl faced him across the table, now decently clad though distinctly ruffled, rather red-cheeked but defiantly smiling.

'This is Caroline,' said Mrs Thornton. 'You've heard me speak of her mother. My oldest, dearest friend.' She turned to the girl. 'We must decide on your surname.' This struck him as an odd remark. He could only mumble a vague but friendly greeting.

The girl had recovered her self-possession. 'I'd better not use my own – or my uncle's. I'd never use *his* anyhow,' she added fiercely. 'I was booked on the coach as "Jennings", but I must drop that now. He may check all the passenger bookings today. Of course I was down as "Mr" Jennings – and *he's* vanished for ever now!'

William liked the way she laughed. But he was utterly mystified.

'Ellen said a young gentleman had gone up to see you,' he told his mother. 'But she thought he'd be gone by now. It was just a message.'

A distant coach sounded its horn. 'Goodness!' cried

his mother. 'I should be down in the kitchen. I'll be back soon,' she promised the girl. 'I must get a quiet word with Mr Thornton. All will be well, dear.' To William she said firmly: '*You* know nothing. You'd better not stay here.' To his disappointment she bundled him out in front of her.

He had come running upstairs eager to pour out the interesting events of the day – Mr Holtby's identity, the plan for the railway, the encounter with Sir Sefton – but all that was now pushed out of his mind. He would have liked to hear the girl's story while his mother dealt with the hungry passengers downstairs. He went, but reluctantly. Still, it might be a good idea to have a wash and change his shirt before meeting Caroline again.

That was not until the family gathered for their own evening meal, often the only chance in the long day to discuss anything together. Even then they were often interrupted. 'It's all go, at the Coach and Horses,' Mrs Thornton used to say. 'Or rather *come* and go, which is even worse.' Now, optimistically, she told Frederick to close the door and shut out the clatter from the public rooms.

William, sitting beside their guest, could not study her face. Only his brother's opposite. Fred was wearing a decidedly daft expression, and William felt a twinge of jealousy. He, after all, had seen her first. He was not going to tell Fred the circumstances. Fred could be very coarse. Just now, though, he was looking quite soft about her. William began to hope that this Caroline would not much care for Fred.

Their mother said: 'You'd better explain to the boys.'

'Very well, my dear.' Mr Thornton eyed them solemnly.

'Listen, both of you. This is strictly confidential.' He was in one of his former butler moods. They became all attention. Fred took his moon-struck gaze off the girl.

Caroline was the daughter of their mother's old friend, Mrs Callender, 'now, sadly, no longer with us. But for family reasons – ' again he used one of his favourite butler phrases, which discouraged questions – 'while Caroline is under our roof she will use the name of Barlow. As if she were your cousin.'

Barlow had been their mother's maiden name, but, as they well knew, she had never had any married sisters. She read their thoughts and interjected softly, 'We were like sisters.'

'That's what *my* mother used to say,' said Caroline.

'So we must help you if we can,' Mr Thornton assured her.

'I want to work for my living. But it's not easy for a girl by herself to find a respectable position. I thought – you have an inn, Mr Thornton – there's always work at an inn, you need girls to wait at table and make beds, scrub floors, wash dishes – I'd do *anything*.'

She spoke vehemently. What were those 'family reasons', William wondered, that had brought her here dressed as a boy? Her arrival was to be kept secret, she was to change her name, pretend to be his cousin. She was obviously afraid she would be followed and dragged home.

'It will be easier,' said his father, 'if you're known as our niece. The servants would be puzzled. They'd wonder why we had suddenly brought in a girl not from these parts – not trained in the work. They'd ask questions and speculate – '

'The last thing I want! But I don't want favouritism. You must treat me like everybody else.'

'We shall,' William's mother promised. 'You shall be employed and paid exactly like the others. But – ' she smiled – 'I should find it hard to treat my old friend's daughter as a stranger. And they won't expect me to. They're good sorts, there'll be no jealousy. They'll help you learn.'

So it was settled. The boys found themselves appointed honorary cousins from that time on.

'You must be quite worn out, poor lamb,' said Mrs Thornton. The meal over, she led Caroline away. There was a small room to spare in the family wing of the building. It would be better than putting her into the big attic where the younger maids slept. They might not welcome a member of their employers' family planted among them.

Fred winked at William as the door closed behind them. 'Nice bit o' muslin,' he said knowingly. Fred liked to put on the airs of a man. He would not have done so if their father had not gone off to tour the inn.

'That's no way to speak of her,' said William.

Fred lifted a heavy paw to clout him, but thought better of it. He remembers *I'm* growing up too, thought William with quiet satisfaction. He went off to check that Mr Holtby had asked for his services for a second day. 'He has,' said his father, 'and told me what's in the wind. You've made a good impression. A very pleasant gentleman he seems. You'd best make sure of a good night's rest.'

There was a light under the door of Number Six when William walked by. Mr Holtby would be already writing up his notes.

Next morning the Twin Roses mail was standing in the

61

yard, spotless and polished, the team clumping out from their stalls to be harnessed. The chaise to carry Mr Holtby up Cragdale would not be at the door for another couple of hours.

Caroline was already at work. She swished out of the kitchen with laden tray and vanished into the room reserved for coachmen and guards. Waterloo Walter would be starting breakfast. William, his devoted admirer, snatched a word with him whenever he could. Hopefully he poked his head into the coffee fumes and aroma of bacon, but the veteran was absorbed in chat with the new waitress.

'Saw your brother yesterday, me dear!'

'My *brother*?' Caroline stared.

'He was your spittin' image, any road.' Waterloo looked up from his plate with a sly expression.

Of course, thought William. She had come on his coach yesterday. He had seen through her disguise if no one else had.

She was bending over the table, mumbling, pleading. The coachman's voice was usually pitched to battle with the wind on the open road. But he seemed to like Caroline. He would not give away her secret. She looked reassured as she turned back towards the kitchen.

Her face lit up as she met William in the doorway. 'Good morning, Master William,' she said primly, copying the other maids. He must tell her not to call him 'Master' if she was to pass as family.

He gave her a friendly grin in passing. He greeted 'Mr Armstrong' and would dearly have loved to question him about her. But he dared not. And soon Waterloo scraped back his chair and strode out to the yard, where Gentleman Joe was fussing over the last formalities of departure and the passengers for Lancashire were climbing aboard. A few minutes later the coach was bowling away up the High Street.

The sun was high when Mr Holtby and William followed in the hired chaise. They drove past Sir Sefton's wrought-iron gates and drew up a mile or two beyond, where a rough track zigzagged steeply upwards to White Beacon Hags. Mr Holtby took out his watch. 'Come back for us at four o'clock,' he told the driver. 'We'll be done by then.'

It was a stiff climb. William was not sorry that the engineer stopped frequently to contemplate the other side of the valley. He unrolled his map, made occasional entries in his notebook, from time to time asked for one of his instruments.

William needed no spy-glass to spot the nick in the skyline opposite, where they had been challenged by Sir Sefton. Mr Holtby was more interested in the hillside about a hundred feet below, where he had spent so much of his time the day before. It was roughly at the same altitude as where they were standing now.

'Yes,' he said with a satisfied grunt. 'This is the spot I had in mind for the other tunnel.' He made a sweeping gesture. 'The line will have come up over Featherbed Moss, through the cutting, then the tunnel under Cragdale Heights, coming out again into the daylight over there. Then I'll bring it over on the bridge and viaduct – and it'll enter the second tunnel *here*.'

'Where we're standing, sir?' William could not keep the awe out of his voice.

'Why not?' Mr Holtby laughed. 'That's what engineering is about. Exact measurements, exact calculations.'

'It's wonderful –'

'If we can dig a tunnel from both ends and join the two

halves in the middle without the variation of an inch – if we can do that in the bowels of the earth – we can surely be accurate in broad daylight!'

Mr Holtby fell to his pottering again. Calculations were all very fine, but there was still much to be checked on the ground. He was tapping rocks, collecting geological samples, scanning the fall of the hillside beneath their feet.

At last he was ready to move on. There would be a more detailed survey, probably with half a dozen assistants, but he foresaw no serious problems. They continued upwards. White Beacon Hags loomed over them, under blue sky and scudding clouds. Once they were over the top Mr Holtby called a halt.

The view beyond the rugged skyline was much what the map had promised. The land tilted steeply down to the west.

'It will be a shorter tunnel this side,' he said, 'and a shorter cutting beyond that. It will save us thousands. And after that – well, judge for yourself. The lie of the land! An easy, straight-forward run!' He was exultant. 'I know the rest of this country, right on to the very mill chimneys of Lancashire. No more bogs, no deep valleys to cross. It's all practicable.'

Today he insisted that William should sit beside him when the provisions were unpacked. He was relaxed, he talked fast and freely. It should now be only routine surveying. He would tell his directors that the scheme could safely go ahead.

Speed was vital. 'They must announce their plan,' he said. 'Draft the bill, lay it before Parliament.'

A railway mania was gripping England. New companies were being formed everywhere, new routes projected. Every rich man wanted to invest in them and make himself richer. A new line across the Pennines would be a money-spinner and if his own directors did not grasp the opportunity others would. It depended on who won the authority from Parliament.

'And Parliament could vote it down, sir? MPs like Sir Sefton?'

'He *could* be an obstacle. Most landowners are only too glad of the money, but I gather that Sir Sefton isn't short of that.'

'They say he's fabulously rich.'

'An inherited fortune from the West Indies, I'm told. He won't be won over with mere compensation money from a railway company. But he has other ambitions. Position. Some of the gentlemen who got him into Parliament won't be pleased if he blocks the railway — *they* want a share of that money. Even the Duke. Dukes can't vote for parliamentary candidates, but they have their own ways of showing their displeasure. When it comes to the pinch, Sir Sefton won't wish to make himself unpopular in the higher circles.'

'You seem to know a lot about him, sir.'

Mr Holtby smiled. 'An engineer has to study more than maps and mathematics. "Know your friends," they say. Sometimes it's more important to know your enemies.'

After that he talked of railway-building in general. William was enthralled, bombarding him with questions which he said were intelligent and answered patiently. 'You're a bright lad,' he commented.

He spoke of the way the new invention was spreading. The French and the Austrians had been building railways now for ten years. Belgium and Holland, Germany and Italy, even Russia were following suit. But the British engineers, said Mr Holtby staunchly, were the best in the world. 'It won't stop with

Europe,' he predicted. 'One day there'll be railways needed in India and South America – the Yankees of course are already building their own, but there'll be openings for the British in every continent. Greater challenges than here, of course – higher mountains, bigger rivers, vast distances.' His eyes shone. William saw the same vision. To a good railway engineer the whole world would lie open.

Mr Holtby stood up, brushing crumbs from his flowered waistcoat. 'The chaise will be back soon,' he said.

They clambered over the ridge again and started down the path. They could not continue their conversation in single file, but William had enough thoughts to fill his mind. When he gazed across the valley it was no longer Cragdale Heights he saw opposite but the ice-bound challenge of some far-off foreign range.

8

'Of course you must write to your aunt,' Mrs Thornton insisted. 'She will be frantic with worry.'

'If my uncle gets the least hint of where I am, he'll tear the town apart to find me.'

'He needn't know. Simply tell them you're safe — with a respectable family. The letter can be posted from London. I can arrange that with one of the guards.'

Caroline was reassured, and glad that she could now set poor Aunt Louisa's mind at rest. She wrote briefly but affectionately, folded the single sheet and blobbed the corners together with sealing wax. Mrs Thornton stuck on one of the new-fangled little black stamps that meant there would be nothing to be paid by the recipient. It was a great convenience, this penny post. Caroline felt she could enter upon her new life with a clear conscience.

'I want to start at the bottom,' she had said firmly.

In fact she found herself starting at the top, constantly running upstairs to answer bells and carry cans of hot water. Then, after helping with the breakfast rush, it was upstairs again to empty grey soapy water into her pail and grovel beside the beds to grope for chamber-pots. After which there were armfuls of crumpled sheets and pillow-cases to be bundled up and taken down to the washhouse, and clean lavender-scented linen to be spread smoothly in their place. At first she seemed always to have one of the older maids breathing down her neck. Mrs Thornton, she was warned, liked everything just so.

It was hard work, but there was a knack in everything, which she was determined to learn. The other girls were good-natured and willing to teach her, once they had summed her up. Some lived in, like Amy the head chambermaid, and Harriet, the cheerful young imp who, in her own phrase, scuttled round the scullery. Others were local, daughters of small shopkeepers and farmers. They all accepted her as Mrs Thornton's niece 'from away'. They asked no awkward questions and did not see her as a rival.

Aunt Matty, as she must now call Mrs Thornton, continued as kindly as she had been from the first. Warm and friendly, she flitted through the rambling inn like some bird – and no less sharp-eyed for slipshod work or forgetfulness. There was not much of those at the Coach and Horses. Caroline made up her mind that she would not let down the standards of the house.

She was a little in awe of Mr Thornton – 'Uncle George'. He looked so very dignified, so gentlemanly, in his bottle-green frock coat. No matter how grand the guest who stepped down from coach or carriage, Uncle George was equal to the occasion. From dukes downwards, they received the appropriate greeting, respectful but never servile. Even the occasional foreigner – not many came to Redford – was welcomed with a phrase or two of French. In his younger days Uncle George had travelled on the Continent as valet to his employer's son, making the Grand

Tour. He was dryly amusing when he recalled those early adventures in France and Italy. He would have Caroline in stitches of laughter. She lost none of her respect but was never again afraid of him.

She saw less, but quite enough, of Frederick. He spent most of his working hours in the stables and yard. He was knowledgeable about horses but, she soon realized, not truly fond of them. He knew how to get the best out of them but had no feeling for them as individual creatures. Post horses had a short working life. The daily mileage, the standard average twelve miles an hour expected from them, could not be kept up for many years. But whereas Uncle George, despite the manifold other matters pressing on his mind, would take endless trouble to find good homes and lighter work for his animals elsewhere, Fred had no scruples about sending them off to the knacker's yard to be slaughtered and fed to the fox-hounds. Caroline found him rough-spoken, grasping and calculating.

She overheard William suggesting that he had been mean with the feed, giving the beasts short measure after their hard day on the roads. They deserved another handful. Fred was outraged.

'Wi' sixty horses in the stalls? Even a handful each, over an' above what's needed! Work it out for yourself, what it costs — you're the scholar, supposed to be! Waste!'

A shrewd head for business, she thought; but no heart for horses.

She liked William, though she saw little of him in those early hectic days. Indeed, she thought, remembering with slight embarrassment the circumstances of their first encounter, I've seen less of William than he has of *me*. But the incident had been so trifling that she did not let the memory trouble her. If it had been Fred, he would not have allowed her to forget it.

At supper on the second evening she listened while William described his day. He was full of this man in Number Six — this Mr Holtby, a railway engineer, it seemed, with this extraordinary notion the coachman had mentioned, to build a line across the hills. To hear William you'd have supposed Mr Holtby was a magician.

She waited till the others had asked their questions and William had poured out his confident replies. When he paused she inquired: 'Are you going out with him tomorrow?'

He shook his head. 'No such luck!' She was sympathetic with him in his obvious disappointment.

There was something likeable about him. She was not sure how much they had in common. She tried him on books, but did not get very far. He had read *Pickwick Papers* and *Oliver Twist*, two of her favourites — but only 'in bits'! How could he start such books and not finish them? She was relieved when she heard the reason.

He had met both the Dickens novels when they first came out in monthly parts. Guests left the separate issues in their bedrooms or the coffee-room and he had learnt to pounce on them when the guests departed. There were one or two months when he had been unlucky and had drawn blank. He had not realized till too late that the missing episodes could have been bought in Redford.

'They're out in book form now. I had them both,' she

70

said sadly, 'but I had to leave them behind. I only brought
– ' She stopped. She would not for the moment offer to
lend him *Pride and Prejudice*. It would cast a shadow on
their dawning friendship if he did not respond to the
subtler humour of Jane Austen.

She went to bed early, even more tired than on the
previous night after the long drive from Eldonby. As she
dragged herself upstairs she saw the light under Mr
Holtby's door. According to William he was likely to
spend half the night writing up his report on the day's
surveying.

He was leaving the next morning. It fell to her to serve
him with breakfast. He seemed a very pleasant gentleman –
he was wearing a different flowered waistcoat, which greatly
appealed to her – and she could understand William's
liking him. He thanked her charmingly for her service and
slipped a generous coin into her hand, which she dropped,
being unprepared for it. William appeared at the doorway,
carrying his bags.

'The London mail will be here in ten minutes, sir.'

Mr Holtby glanced through the window at the cloudless sky. 'Pity! It would have been a grand day for the hills.'

'Yes, sir.' William sounded wistful.

'But we'll meet again. And if you're still of the same
mind we'll have to see if anything can be done.'

A horn sounded in the distance. Fred could be heard
in the yard, marshalling the change of horses. Upstairs
Amy's powerful voice was demanding: 'Where's that girl?'
Caroline bobbed to Mr Holtby and fled.

9

Mr Holtby had gone, Caroline Callender had come. Otherwise, as the summer wore on, William's life became uneventful again.

He resumed his role of odd-job boy at the Coach and Horses. This girl who had come from nowhere fitted better into the establishment, he thought bitterly, than he did himself. No one was ever wondering, what can we give her to do? Anyhow, Caroline would always have found something. She was not one to stand about. And his mother was making sure that she had a thorough training in every branch of domestic work.

'She may never need to earn her bread this way, but what she learns here will always stand her in good stead. Some day she'll marry and have a household of her own to run.'

There was no such programme ahead of William. Now that he had left school he was expected to 'make himself useful' – a blanket term, vague as a blanket in a dark room. His father was busy with more pressing matters. He would call to Fred, 'Get your brother to give you a hand!' or to William, 'Fred will show you how to do that!' The boys were reluctant workmates. It was seldom a harmonious partnership.

William loved horses but until now he had had little

close contact with them individually. The strict timetable of their working life gave little chance for affectionate stroking and nuzzling. It was all brisk harnessing and unharnessing, feeding and watering. His own jobs were mainly mucking out, sweeping and shovelling mounds of steaming dung, swilling the cobbles, heaving bales of straw and hay. In handling the beasts themselves he had still to gain confidence. Fred would jeer at him and slap the horse's massive hindquarters. 'Gerrover, dam' ye!' And add contemptuously, to William: 'Got to show 'em who's master, or ye'll never be any good.'

If anything ever happened to their father — God forbid — and Fred took over, it would be a poor look-out for William.

The girl's arrival did nothing to promote brotherly love. She and William shared the same sense of fun. Without uttering a syllable they could convey things that were best not put into words. Fred would intercept their glances and become suspicious — often with good reason — and his temper was not improved.

Gradually William formed a picture of Caroline's previous existence, though it was seldom referred to in the family circle. By a hint here and a hint there he learnt more about her odious uncle and ineffective aunt. He guessed that his parents knew more than they let on. But it was their nature to support adult authority and they would not undermine it in the eyes of their own sons. They were sympathetic to Caroline but sad that she had been driven to this drastic revolt.

Fred, though strongly attracted to her, could not

73

entirely approve of her behaviour. Once, discussing her with William, he confided: 'I don't mind telling you, when she first turned up, I thought she was in trouble.'

'She *was* in trouble.'

'Not that sort. *Real* trouble. Starting a baby. Not married.'

'*Caroline?*' William was horrified.

'Why not? Plenty o' girls younger . . .' Fred prided himself on being worldly-wise. 'An' with her looks! Still, I guessed wrong, so we haven't that to worry about. We've never had a scandal at the Coach an' Horses. But you've got to admit, she's a bit of a wild 'un, runnin' off like that. She'll steady down,' he concluded. 'Only needs a man to knock the nonsense out o' her.'

Fred spoke as though she were a filly, merely needing someone like himself to break her in. William made no answer.

As the days went by she became more relaxed. Sometimes he heard her singing as she bustled about in some adjoining room. Once he murmured shyly, 'You're looking a lot better than when you arrived.' He meant, even prettier.

'Did I look ill?'

'Not ill. Unhappy.'

'Did I?' She admitted nothing. 'So do you, sometimes.'

He found himself telling her about Mr Holtby. If only this railway scheme came off, if the bill got through Parliament, if Mr Holtby came back, if Mr Holtby . . . He could not keep the note of yearning out of his voice.

'And if Parliament throws out the bill?' she asked.

'He'll be building railways somewhere else.'

74

'You'd leave home?' There was dismay in her voice. Cool of her, he thought afterwards – since it was what *she* had done? True, the cases were different.

'There's nothing for me here,' he said. 'I'm not cut out for the inn trade. And it's quite right for a boy to go off and seek his fortune.'

'But not – ' She stopped, biting her lip. Forcing a lighter tone, she went on, 'I hope you won't go yet awhile.'

'Not much chance.' Mr Holtby had said complimentary things, but he already had a young assistant, though he had not brought him to Redford. This youth's apprenticeship had still a year to run. 'He wouldn't want me at the same time. There's so much to learn – and that means so much to teach. Once the work gets under way he'll have to concentrate his mind on the day-to-day problems. No, my best hope is in a railway here. If I was on the spot I'm sure he'd find me things to do. Maybe not every day. He'd ask Dad if he could spare me for this or that. "*Spare*" me!' William laughed bitterly.

'And then you wouldn't have to leave home!' Her anxious tone became more cheerful.

'It would be a start anyhow. Mr Holtby wouldn't have to commit himself. There'd be no legal papers to sign – I expect my parents would feel easier about it. Half a loaf,' he said philosophically. 'Better than no bread.'

'Much better. Papa used to say – ' She stopped. She seldom referred to her parents – it was a sad subject, but he guessed they were often in her thoughts.

'What did he say?'

'There were poor men in the parish – work was hard

75

to find. They'd ask his advice, especially if they'd been offered something without much pay or prospects. "Take it," he'd say, "and then *make yourself indispensable*." '

'Is that *your* motto here?'

She flushed. 'Your mother's been good to me. I'd do anything not to disappoint her.'

'It's a good motto. I'll adopt it if Mr Holtby gives me half a chance.'

Fred bellowed for him from the stableyard. He ran. It was not often he and Caroline managed so long a conversation.

For the present he could only buckle down to the humdrum jobs given him. The railway project was seldom mentioned at the Coach and Horses. Very likely, people said, nothing would come of it. If it ever was built it would run north of Redford and the nearest station would be miles away. Life here would be little affected.

'When a matter gets to Parliament,' said Mr Thornton, 'delays can be endless.' Both as a butler and now as an innkeeper he had often heard the gentry discuss the leisurely debating of Lords and Commons. 'We'll hear nothing for months,' he said.

He was not often wrong. This time he was. Only a few days later Caroline came racing across the yard into the stables where William was busy with his usual malodorous tasks.

'Look out!' he yelled, saving her in the nick of time from measuring her length on the slippery cobbles. She stopped, grateful for his steadying hand. She waved a newspaper.

'Read this!' she cried. 'That parson left it in his room.'

It was yesterday's *Times*. She pointed to the parliamentary report. A private bill for another railway line to link Yorkshire with Lancashire had passed both Houses, received the royal assent, and was now law.

He could have seized her hands and danced round with her, but it was not a good place for such celebrations.

Nobody else was convulsed with excitement at the news. 'It will be a long time,' William's father still obstinately predicted, 'before we see much doing in this neighbourhood.' The railway would have to climb up from the flat country and it would be months before it reached the higher ground that it must cross. It would be many a long day before Mr Holtby's pleasant face would be seen in Redford.

Again Mr Thornton was mistaken. By the next mail from London came a letter.

'He'll be here tomorrow night!' For once Mr Thornton's dignified features were disarranged by something like excitement. 'He wishes to reserve Number Six for an indefinite period. And a smaller room, within call if possible, for his young assistant. Mr Spaxton.'

'Number Seven,' said Mrs Thornton smartly.

'Did he mention me?' William inquired.

His father's dark eyebrows arched with incredulous disapproval. In his butlering days those majestic eyebrows had often rebuked an ill-bred guest who showed ignorance of correct procedure in a gentleman's establishment.

'And why should he, my boy?'

'I just thought — '

'This is a business letter, not an exchange of family inquiries.' Mr Thornton frowned at the document. 'He looks forward to receiving the same excellent service as heretofore. You, I would hope, were part of that service.'

'I hope so too.'

'And will be again, if required.' That sounded promising. His father appeared willing to let him work for the engineer as before. But would the presence of this Spaxton leave much scope for William?

Mr Holtby wrote from London. No doubt he had been there to canvass the support of MPs and peers for the bill. His married sister lived in London, and, being himself a childless widower, he made her house his base between his engineering contracts. William wondered if he had tackled Sir Sefton Creevey for his vote, but could not imagine that he had met with much encouragement in that quarter.

What did that matter now? The bill had gone through. No one could stop the project. And Mr Holtby would be on the coach from London tomorrow night.

10

William was waiting to seize Mr Holtby's bags as soon as the guard lifted them out of the boot.

The engineer's eyes twinkled at the eagerness of his welcome. 'You didn't expect me back here so soon?'

'Hardly, sir.'

'This is William, Peter. My assistant, William – Peter Spaxton.'

A lanky youth swung down from the coach with outthrust hand. He had a pronounced limp, William noticed. Mr Holtby had spared him the rough walking of that original survey.

'Everybody seemed to think, sir, that you'd be making for the place where the line will start. But I explained to Dad that you wouldn't have to – you might want to take advantage of the season and the long days, and make a beginning in the high country before the winter made things difficult – '

The appearance of a smiling Mr Thornton in the doorway cut short William's chatter.

'My son gave us a lecture over supper,' he explained, 'how an engineer by his wonderful calculations can start a tunnel from both ends at once and guarantee on their meeting precisely in the middle!'

Mr Holtby laughed as he was intended to, but backed

William loyally. 'He was quite right, Mr Thornton. Your boy has a very sound notion of what engineering is about. We shall probably work on several sections of the line simultaneously, to save time and fit in with weather conditions. But I think I can promise you that we shall finish up with one continuous line.' They trooped upstairs. He walked into his former bedroom and looked round it with approval. 'Excellent! I fancy this will be my headquarters until the spring. And where better?'

Where indeed, thought William? Obviously life was to be transformed, not only for himself but for everyone in Redford.

Strangers would be swarming into the town. There were not nearly enough local men available for the labour that would be needed. The influx would bring business for the Redford shops, the alehouses and market-stalls, the cobblers and blacksmiths and men of every trade.

When Mr Holtby came down to supper he soon settled any doubts about William's involvement.

'The first thing I must ask you, Mr Thornton — can you hire me, tomorrow, a good quiet horse suitable for these hills?'

'Certainly, sir. No difficulty.'

'And another — a stout pony would do — for Mr Spaxton?'

'By all means.'

'And can you spare me your son for the morning?'

'Of course.'

'He'd better be mounted too.'

'He shall be, Mr Holtby.'

'Until the work starts I can't be certain — but I fancy

I may be glad of his assistance quite frequently. I'll have gangs of men working in different places; that means sending orders to and fro, often over rocks and rough ground where a horse can't go. I'll need a lad who can nip about on his own two feet – '

Which Peter Spaxton can't, thought William, straining his ears in the background.

'And so,' went on Mr Holtby, 'if agreeable to you – and of course to the lad himself – '

'My lads do as I bid them,' said Mr Thornton grandly. 'The convenience of our customers is our only aim.' He relaxed into an easier tone. 'William will be happy to help in any way. He talks of nothing but your project.'

So the next morning, after breakfast, the three of them mounted and rode off.

The first thing, Peter told William, was to choose a site where the workmen could be accommodated when they began to arrive.

'But there's nowhere up here,' cried William, 'nothing!'

'They don't expect anything. These fellows are tough – and rough. They'll sleep out while the weather holds. Then they'll rig up their own shacks and shelters.'

'We thought they'd take lodgings in Redford – only we couldn't imagine where they'd find enough beds – '

'They wouldn't. Mr Holtby wants a thousand men. At least.'

'A *thousand!*'

'And if they found beds in Redford,' said Mr Holtby, 'who'd fancy this long tramp up and down – as well as a sixteen-hour day?'

It was quite usual, he assured William, for these men

to build themselves a sort of shanty town handy for the site. They had been doing so since the first navigation canals were dug, years ago. You couldn't beat the 'navvies' – especially the Irishmen. They were strong as oxes. They flocked over to England because there was nothing for them in their own country. They had no homes in England anyhow. They would sleep rough and put up with any conditions if the money was good.

Beyond the brow of the hill the road petered out. Featherbed Moss lay green in front of them. The desolate hills stood round, dotted with their weather-beaten rocks, Mad Woman's Stones, Lost Lass, and the other landmarks.

Mr Holtby turned in his saddle, pointing to the left. 'I thought here, Peter.' He urged his horse along a narrow track that ribboned away through the heather.

There was a level stretch of firm ground at the base of Dagger Stones, comfortably clear of the marsh. A little stream glinted bright silver through the grass.

'Pure water to fill their kettles,' said the engineer with approval. 'Dry heather yonder, for kindling. A good spot over there that would take our covered waggon.'

Surely, thought William in alarm, he did not mean to forsake the comfort of the Coach and Horses? But no, it seemed that the waggon would be only for daytime use – shelter for all the writing and calculating – a kind of office and a place where they could eat their luncheon out of the wind. Half a dozen workmen would manhandle it over the rough ground from the road.

Looking about him, he was more conscious than ever before of the strewn boulders and the tussocks of coarse grass. Ways would have to be cleared and levelled for the carts to pass to and fro with their loads. Riding horses would be of limited use here. He could see why his own strong legs would be so useful for errands. Poor Peter Spaxton would be badly handicapped.

He wondered how, with such a disability, Peter could ever have obtained his apprenticeship. Before the day was over he had learnt the answer. It was not a long-standing handicap, but the result of an injury caused a year ago by the overturning of a waggon. The surgeon had done his best, but the leg would never be the same again. Some engineers would have made that an excuse to terminate the agreement. Matthew Holtby was not that sort of man.

Now, while William held the horses, the engineer and his apprentice crouched over map and notebook spread out upon a flat rock. Peter had obviously studied all this paperwork before. Holtby was identifying the actual features referred to, explaining the problems they either created or solved.

William could be only an interested eavesdropper, making what he could of their technical jargon, envious of Peter's knowledge and awed by the way he gave his opinion when invited. Given the same chance to learn he must make himself as good.

Holtby folded the map at last and stood up. 'That's all we can do up here this morning. The next jobs are waiting for us in Redford.'

'In Redford, sir?'

'We're going to need carts and draught horses to pull them. A hundred horses at least, maybe two hundred

83

before we're done. I must see what the local farmers can offer. Talk to the dealers. Some of my foremen may be here by tonight. And when the navvies start trickling in they'll have to be formed into gangs.'

'Are you really going to need a thousand?'

'More, probably.'

'But how do you *find* them?'

Holtby laughed. 'They find me. The word gets round. When they get here lots of them will be penniless. The company can't afford to pay them for doing nothing, so we must get the first arrivals started on something that won't be a waste of effort.'

'Like a track wide enough to take carts,' Peter suggested, 'along the edge of this bog. Then, when we start excavating, we can bring along the spoil and dump it for the causeway.'

'Lucky,' said the engineer cheerfully, 'that we can go straight ahead here, without waiting for permissions.' Seeing William's questioning look he went on: 'We've cleared it with the Duke. He's been all for the scheme from the start. He helped us a lot to get the bill through Parliament. He's going to do very well out of it himself.'

And the Duke, William remembered, owned all this land up to the western skyline of Cragdale Heights. As they rode off the moor he turned in his saddle and glanced back at that ridge, rising green and grey in the midday sun. And like statues, posed against the scudding cloud, three figures stood motionless, watching them ride away.

II

The fear that had haunted Caroline during her first days at Redford had faded gradually with the passing of time.

Originally it had seemed almost too easy. Was it too good to be true? Her escape from the house, the straightforward coach journey, the unbelievably warm welcome from the Thorntons . . . How long could she expect such luck to last?

Perhaps she had allowed Uncle Daniel to intimidate her. She had built him up in her mind as a sinister ogre who would always triumph in the end, liable to spring out of a stage trapdoor like the villain in a Christmas pantomime. After living under his roof she knew what an important personage he was. Such a man would never tamely accept her disappearance. He would seek ways and means to track her down. He might advertise, have handbills printed, hire men to make inquiries, even offer a reward, as though she were a thief.

But nothing happened. If he had picked up any clue about her coach journey he would have appeared in Redford long ago. But only old Waterloo seemed to have seen through her disguise, and he had not betrayed her. Perhaps the letter to her aunt, purporting to come from London, had done the trick. Finding a runaway in London was always difficult. Finding someone who had not run there

– she could have hugged herself with glee – would be more difficult still.

As he had obviously picked up no evidence straight after her escape there could be no risk now of his connecting her with Redford. Neither the town nor the Thorntons had ever been mentioned in his hearing. She had never thought of them herself until she began to rack her brains for a refuge. There *was* no connection with Redford, except of course the Twin Roses coach, itself just one of a dozen different mail services passing through Eldonby every day to places all over the country.

But the Twin Roses *did* constitute a link. One morning she was reminded of the fact with a shock that almost stopped her heart.

Not all passengers intending to take the early coaches spent the previous night at the inn. Some lived close by. Some had been staying with friends. Such people would drive up just in time for one of Mrs Thornton's famous breakfasts before their journey. On this occasion, as Caroline approached the coffee-room, she heard Lancashire voices, indeed Eldonby voices. Dangerously familiar. Voices she remembered from her aunt's drawing-room.

She stopped in the doorway. Mr and Mrs Dixon would recognize her. They would tell Uncle Daniel. And then she must be gone from here within twenty-four hours, a fugitive again. Where in the world could she hope to find another family like the Thorntons?

Ellen, hurrying out with an empty tray, almost collided with her. 'Oh, *there* you are! The couple in the window are hollerin' for their hot rolls – they're catchin' the Twin Roses in twenty minutes. See to them, will you?'

Caroline ran to the kitchen in panic. It was the Dixons at the table in the bow-window. She *could* not serve them. She made for Mrs Thornton, who was directing operations with her usual unflustered efficiency. She saw Caroline's desperation.

'What *is* it, dear? You look — '

Caroline whispered. Mrs Thornton grasped the situation.

'Leave it to me.' She raised her voice. 'I want you to run across to the hen-house. Pick me out six really fine eggs, brown ones, must be brown, mind. *I'll* see the lady and gentleman get their hot rolls.'

Caroline fled across the yard. The problem of finding the six large brown eggs did not worry her. The larder was full of eggs anyhow. One of the other girls had just collected them. She had her excuse to keep out of the coffee-room.

She did not venture back till she heard the babble of people boarding the coaches, Waterloo's voice, Gentleman Joe packing luggage into the boot. She saw the backs of the passengers as they crowded forward. She slipped back by the side door and ran upstairs to peep down from one of the vacated bedrooms.

The Eldonby voices floated up to her. 'A remarkable resemblance!' Mrs Dixon was saying in her emphatic way.

For the second time Caroline stiffened with alarm.

'So *I* thought,' boomed the portly Mr Dixon. 'Nay, I could have sworn. Even to the white patch!'

'But our cat has *two* white patches. Otherwise, the living image!'

Now Caroline was shaking with the uncontrollable

laughter of relief. The Dixons got into the coach. Gentleman Joe mounted to the box and lifted his bugle to sound a few notes for their triumphant departure. But no music could have matched the triumph in Caroline's heart as the coach wheeled out into the High Street.

It had been a near thing. And it could happen again. But thanks to the strict time-keeping of the mails there need be only two brief predictable periods of danger, the arrivals and the departures of the Eldonby coach. If she were alert at those times all should be well.

Even that anxiety practically died in the fresh excitement over the railway project, which soon gripped the entire town. Strange faces filled the streets. She herself, once noticeable as a newcomer, no longer attracted attention. William told her of the ramshackle colony that had sprung up on the moors. Despite the long hours the men worked some would straggle down into Redford, filling the cheaper alehouses and reeling about the streets, singing in uncouth accents when decent folk had gone to bed. They did not trouble the Coach and Horses. They were not too far gone to remember that it was where Mr Holtby lodged and they did not want to lose their jobs.

Life at the Coach and Horses underwent its own changes. Important gentlemen came to see Mr Holtby. Directors of his company, sub-contractors, merchants and manufacturers who might be affected by the construction of the railway, even newspaper men. They drank prodigiously of the best wines in Mr Thornton's cellars — though a few on principle demanded tea at all times or purest water from the hills. They mostly smoked like chimneys, surrounding themselves with a pungent haze from their cigars. They talked in loud confident voices (sometimes Caroline was disagreeably reminded of Uncle Daniel and his cronies) but they would drop into furtive whispers when their business called for secrecy.

It was all very good for trade, Mr Thornton admitted, but Caroline suspected that in some cases they were not the kind of customer he preferred. There were even one or two that Mrs Thornton rebuked in a polite but tight-lipped way for behaving with undue familiarity to her maids. She gave Caroline a discreet hint to give these gentlemen a wide berth. But Caroline had already been warned by Ellen and by the protective William. She avoided dark passages and jovial gentlemen.

Mr Holtby she liked immensely. Though she did not share William's technical interests she could understand his admiration for the engineer. She liked his pleasant young assistant and felt sorry for his lameness. She had only one grudge against them and their wonderful scheme: they took up so much of William's time. But it was what the boy wanted and she must be glad for his sake.

Apart from that, she could have wished that it was his brother whose services they required. At Eldonby her real cousin had been rather dull but at least harmless, a bore with whom she had nothing in common. Fred, her pretended cousin, she found equally dull but hardly harmless. I suppose we do have one interest in common, she thought wryly, and that's *me*. As a normal girl she need scarcely apologize for taking an interest in herself, but Fred's interest was uninvited and unwelcome.

She tried to avoid being left alone with him. Not easy, when you lived under the same roof, and no easier when his young brother was out so much. Now William was quite a different proposition. For one thing, they were the same age. For one thing . . .

Nevertheless, she felt guilty about her distaste for Fred. The Thorntons had been so good to her, it seemed ungrateful to harbour even an unspoken criticism of any of them. Mrs Thornton, now warmly enshrined in her heart as 'Aunt Matty', she admired beyond measure. So competent, so firm but so fair in her management, so human with her rare flashes of humour, deferring to her husband when appropriate, yet holding her own in a way unimaginable to Aunt Louisa . . . For Mr Thornton Caroline felt unbounded respect. The Coach and Horses was his little kingdom, he ruled with dignity but was never a tyrant. She loved his dry reminiscences of early days abroad and as butler in a great house, dealing with difficult characters in the servants' hall and awkward guests upstairs.

Her only criticism of William was his absorption in the railway. Did he never think of anything else, she wondered crossly?

One evening at supper he was bubbling with even more enthusiasm than usual. They were making such good progress on the cutting below Cragdale Heights that Mr Holtby was starting the tunnel beyond. They had begun blasting that day.

'We heard,' said his mother. 'We thought it was thunder in the hills.'

'I really must walk up and see the works,' said Caroline.

'Everyone in the town seems to. Perhaps Sunday afternoon, if it's fine.'

It was her turn for the Sunday off allowed to the maids once a month. Most of them used it to visit their parents a few miles away. She had been wondering what to do with her own free day.

'You can't go up there on your own!' Fred exclaimed. She wished she had not mentioned the idea.

'Why ever not?'

'There's – ' he hesitated – 'all sorts up there. Men selling liquor – and the navvies drinking it. Sunday's about their only chance. No decent girl – ' Fred stopped, speechless with alarm and indignation.

Before Caroline could answer she felt an urgent pressure from William's hand beneath the table. He said, very casually: 'Fred's right. They're a rough lot. I'll walk up with you.'

This did not suit Fred. 'You'd be safer with me.'

'But you can't explain anything to her,' retorted William.

'That's what I'd really like,' she said.

'I know I'm not an engineer,' said Fred scornfully. 'Are *you*, William?'

'I can tell her anything she wants to know.'

'One of those navvies could lay you flat with one hand!'

'Course he could,' William admitted. 'But he wouldn't. They all know me. They know I'm one of Mr Holtby's assistants. Anyhow, I wouldn't take Caroline near the shanties. She can see everything from the top of the hill.'

'Perhaps you boys could *both* go?' their mother

suggested with rather less than her usual insight.

There was an awkward pause. The suggestion did not appeal to any of the three. 'Oh, I've plenty of things to *do*,' said Fred in a lordly tone, and flung out of the room. Caroline just hoped it would not rain on Sunday.

12

It did not rain. It was a superb September afternoon, with only a rare cloud shadow drifting like a grey wing across the moors.

By the time they reached the brow of the hill they had enjoyed the longest private conversation since her coming. She had poured out the tragic story of her parents' illnesses and deaths, and the period that had followed at Eldonby. It was a glorious relief. William was a sympathetic listener. For him too, he admitted, it was a relief. 'Dad said not to badger you with questions. But now you've told me . . .'

She cried out at the landscape laid before them. The shanty town lay in the foreground, a haze of blue smoke hovering over a hundred smouldering fires. From the first week, he explained, the Irishmen had started cutting turves of peat and stacking them to dry for fuel. He pointed out the covered waggon, standing apart, which served Mr Holtby as an office. He indicated the rough new track worn by the carts which brought spoil from the cutting to dump in the bog for a causeway. On this Sabbath afternoon all was silent but for the cries of grouse and curlew.

'The men are asleep or drunk – or both,' he said. 'If they stay in their camp what else is there to do?'

They worked sixteen hours a day throughout the week. She could guess how heavy the work was. The hours did not particularly shock her. The children in mills and mines worked nearly as long. So, in his own way, did Mr Holtby himself. He had told William that Mr Brunel, the very prince of engineers, might work up to twenty hours before he slept.

The navvies, William explained to her, swarmed to the construction sites because of the wages. These muscular giants could earn twenty pounds a week. They could send home a decent sum to their families in Ireland. There, all too often, there was nothing at all.

He took her across the breezy summit of Dagger Stones. Below them the curving track of the projected line was already roughly levelled and marked with posts. He pointed up the steep-sided cutting the men had excavated as it approached Cragdale Heights. Among the rocks up there, he said, he and Mr Holtby had been sitting when Sir Sefton Creevey had appeared, told them they had crossed the boundary on to his land, and ordered them off.

'I don't think we've anything to fear from him now, though — only he's a man who hates to be beaten. The Duke's glad of the money, but Sir Sefton doesn't need any more. He's brought so much back from Jamaica, he expects to have everything his own way here, same as there. He thinks money can buy anything.'

Caroline knew someone else with that outlook. Mr Holtby, however, had been lucky. With a duke on his side, and so many local people who thought a railway would be good for business, he had seen his bill pass through

Parliament, and now he could snap his fingers at a single objector like Sir Sefton.

William was telling her how many thousands of tons of earth had been shifted to make the cutting. 'And now we're getting to the tunnel we shall be up against solid rock.'

'How will they – ' She stopped, remembering. 'Of course, they're using gunpowder.'

They should make good progress, he thought. When the bad weather came they would be protected from it, working underground. Only, out in the open, drifting snow might hamper the carts carrying away the rocks and rubble. But somehow, depend on it, Mr Holtby would push on. Speed was vital. The sooner the line was open, the sooner would the money begin to flow for the promoters who had put up the capital.

They filed along the edge of the embankment. The cutting grew deeper with every step they took.

He turned. 'Like to see the entrance to the tunnel?'

'Is it all right?' she asked doubtfully.

'Oh, it's safe enough – sound as a rock!' He laughed.

'I mean, are we allowed?'

'*I* am,' he reminded her proudly. 'They'll not be working there, not Sunday afternoon.'

'I'd love to see it.'

'Come on then. Watch your step.'

He began to slither down the bank, stopping at intervals to hold out a steadying hand.

'I'm all right,' she panted impatiently.

She reached the bottom without slipping. Ahead, the

mouth of the tunnel loomed black. It was jagged. 'Like when the blacksmith makes a mess of taking your tooth out,' he said cheerfully.

She shuddered. 'Ugh!'

'Peter says, when it's finished, it will be all neat and smooth with dressed stone. Like a grand archway. The sides of the cutting will grass over again, it'll all blend with the hillside.'

It was an easy stroll up to the entrance. The gradient was gentle. A locomotive would make nothing of it, William assured her confidently, though as yet he had never set eyes on one.

'Those barrels!' She exclaimed, seeing them stacked just inside the entrance. 'Are those gunpowder?'

'Must be.' His brows knitted. 'There ought by rights to be someone watching 'em. Even in a desolate spot like this. Mr Holtby would have something to say! I expect the foreman posted a look-out and the fellow's got drunk or just taken himself off.' On their way back, he said, he'd find some responsible person at the shanties and tell him.

'Do you have Chartists in Redford?' she asked.

'Chartists?' He stared at her. *He's surprised that I've even* heard *of Chartists,* she thought with a little stab of irritation – even William could irritate her sometimes.

'There were a lot in Eldonby,' she said calmly. 'They're strong in all the Lancashire mill-towns. Uncle Daniel used to go purple in the face. He wouldn't have the word mentioned in his house.'

'I don't think we've any of the violent kind. Plenty who say that working men should have votes. But no talk of red revolution or anything like that. No smuggling of arms or secret drilling on the moors. I should think the Newport business put an end to all that sort of thing.'

The Newport business was still fresh in people's minds. Thousands of Chartist supporters had marched on the little Monmouthshire town, troops had opened fire and killed some of them, and their leaders had been transported for life as convicts to Australia.

'I wonder if it has,' she said. 'All this gunpowder might be a great temptation.'

'You're right. We must speak to someone as we go home.'

'Carefully though. People hate to be put in the wrong. I should wait till you see Mr Holtby this evening.'

'I will.' He sounded relieved.

They had been standing just inside the mouth of the tunnel, where the barrels were stacked in the shelter of the overhanging rock. Now they advanced cautiously into the gloom. Suddenly she laid her hand on his arm. He jumped, startled. 'Isn't that someone talking – outside?' she whispered.

He listened. 'You're right. P'raps they followed us.'

'Oh! Shall we get into trouble?'

'Course not.' But he too kept his voice down. 'We've a perfect right. *They* mayn't have. They may have got girls with them.'

She strained her ears. Heavy footsteps were crunching on the levelled ground outside. She could make out two men's voices. When their approaching figures became visible in the sunshine there was no sign of anyone else.

William whispered again, his breath hot against her ear. 'I've seen these fellows before. Sir Sefton's gamekeeper. And that prize-fighter.' She shuddered, remembering his description of them. '*They've* no right,' he went on hoarsely. 'It's not their side of the hill. They're up to something.'

There was soon no doubt of that. The men stopped in the entrance, their massive figures silhouetted against the daylight. The gamekeeper would be the one with the gun under his arm.

'Eleven barrels,' said the other. 'Should be enough for a grand little firework show.'

The keeper grunted. 'Reckon so.'

'Set the work back a while!'

'Ay.'

'Shall I break one of 'em open?'

'No need.'

'But ye'll want loose powder, surely, to lay a trail?'

'Got enough in my powder-horn. It'll reach the distance. Then we'll just need a spark and a flame. The whole lot will go up like Kingdom Come.' William's fingers tightened on her arm.

The men were quietly pottering. The keeper straightened up and spoke again. 'There, John. A little heap by the barrel. Plenty left for the trail. We'll be over the ridge afore anyone gets here.' Their footsteps began to back away.

'We've got to get out of here!' said William.

She did not need telling. It would be death to stay where they were, useless to move further into the tunnel – it went on for only a few more yards. If the explosion did not blow them to pieces it would bury them alive behind the fall of rock. They could only race after the receding figures.

The men were moving slowly, the keeper stooping as he carefully sprinkled powder from his horn. He glanced up in alarm as they appeared.

'Be off wi' ye, young rascals! Could ha' been killed! Do yer sweetheartin' somewhere else!'

It was not the moment to correct his false impression. She brushed past him thankfully. But the other man, Battling John, thrust out an immense arm and grabbed William. 'Ye've not seen us!' he said fiercely. 'Mind that, ye've not *seen* us! Say a word, I'll seek ye out and break every bone in yer body!'

At this point a new voice was heard. From the top of the bank came a lusty shout with an Irish ring. 'Hey! What's on, down there?' She saw a gigantic youth against the sky. He wore the round woollen cap and moleskin trousers of a navvy.

The prize-fighter glared up and bellowed: 'Get back! If ye don't want to get hurt!'

The young Irishman took no notice. He came plunging wildly down the side of the cutting.

She added her own warning, shrill and urgent. 'They're blowing up the gunpowder!' But he could not check himself. He was slithering, tumbling, down the slope.

'Run for it!' cried the gamekeeper. 'All on ye!' She heard the scrape of the match, a little crackle, a sputter. A thin thread of sparkling fire went snaking back towards the tunnel.

'Get *back!*' Caroline screamed to the youth — quite vainly.

As William seized her arm and forced her into a run she saw the Irish youth stumble down on to the floor of the cutting. He was dancing like a demon, trying to stamp out the powder train. But the glittering bead of fire escaped his boots and raced on towards the tunnel mouth, inexorably.

'Get down!' yelled William, and pulled her roughly to the ground beside him.

They flattened themselves just as the explosion came, echoing thunderously between the embankments, filling the air with stench and smoke and flying stone.

13

Blinded and breathless, they sprawled there until the last rumbling died and the patter of fragments ceased. 'Are you all right?' she gasped.

'Are *you*?'

They picked themselves up. The dust-haze thinned. The gash in the hillside yawned.

The youth lay still. His woollen cap had blown off. His hair was curly, rust-red.

Their own fear went. The two men had vanished. There would be no more explosions. They hurried back, stumbling over scattered lumps of rock and splintered barrel staves. The youth stared up at them, eyes blue as the sky. 'The divils!' he groaned. 'Me leg's smashed.' His trousers were in tatters, darkening every moment with the blood that welled out.

'We must *do* something,' said Caroline.

But what could they do? The fellow looked scarcely older than themselves but he was a positive giant. At least, thought William desperately, they must staunch the bleeding. He slipped out of his coat and tore off a shirt-sleeve for a bandage. One of them must go for help. He could run quicker than Caroline in her skirt, but could he leave her?

He was spared the decision. It was now mid-afternoon

and more people had come strolling up from the town. The previously empty moor was alive with figures. Besides the unkempt navvies, startled from sleep by the explosion, there were the Redford townsfolk in their Sunday finery, all top hats and bonnets, picking their way gingerly through the tussocky grass and the heather. The explosion must have rocked the hills.

William and Caroline were thrust aside. The workmen were used to accidents. 'Ye'll be all right,' they assured the Irish boy. 'We'll have ye to the doctor in no time.' Two men dashed off to the shanties and came back with a door taken off its hinges to serve as a stretcher. One of the foremen had taken charge. He sent someone to arrange for a cart to come up the track. He spotted William.

'Did you see what happened, lad?'

'I did, Mr McDougal.' William poured out his story, Caroline supported him.

'You mean you know these men, Thornton?'

'Yes. One's well known in these parts. Battling John — he was a prize-fighter, but he works now for Sir Sefton Creevey. The other was Gibbon. He's head gamekeeper to Sir Sefton.'

'You know them too, miss?'

'I've not seen them before. But I'd know them again.'

'Then Mr Holtby will get the law on 'em. Depend on it. All that gunpowder. Young Molony might have been blown to blazes.' Mr McDougal turned again to William. 'And when did you first see the men?' William began to explain. 'You saw them at the mouth of the tunnel?' the foreman exclaimed. 'You were there before they arrived?'

'Yes.'

'And where was Molony? Hadn't he stopped you and told you not to go near the tunnel?'

William felt a warning kick on his ankle. Caroline's long Sunday skirt enabled her to transmit the warning signal unnoticed. Of course! The unfortunate Irish boy had been the look-out, watching the gunpowder dump. He had paid for his slackness. He should not suffer for it any further. William began to shape his account accordingly. He was rewarded by Caroline's approving smile.

The injured youth was carried off by his workmates. William and Caroline followed and, with a dozen or two sympathizers, walked down into Redford behind the cart in which he was placed. They must know how badly hurt he was before they could go home.

In all its fifty years Redford's little hospital had scarcely seen so much excitement. A farm accident or a house fire had been its most dramatic emergencies. Since the start of the railway construction there had been an increase in serious injuries but nothing to match this explosion. The surgeon had been sent for and arrived at full gallop. The ancient bloodstains on his tailcoat were evidence of his long experience. He looked almost disappointed to hear that only a single person awaited his attentions.

'Powerful young fellow, though! He'll take some holding down, this one. Still . . .' He looked round the clustered workmen. 'Plenty of you. And I'm reckoned a fast worker.'

William shuddered. Mr Shawcross, it was said, could take your leg off as soon as look at you. People were only too thankful for his speed. The swifter the knife and saw, the shorter the agony. Not much else you could do for the patient except pour strong liquor down his throat, shove a gag between his teeth, and hold him down until the ghastly job was done.

William had never witnessed such an operation and did not want to. He must certainly get Caroline away. She was white as a sheet, whiter certainly than the soiled sheets of the infirmary. But thankfully, as he edged her towards the door, he heard the surgeon's verdict.

'Nay, it'll not come to that. I can save the leg.' He began to give brisk instructions.

As the friends left, Mr Holtby arrived and rushed past them into the building. There seemed nothing left to do but return to the Coach and Horses. News of the explosion was now all over the town and William's mother would be anxious about their own safety.

For news of the young Irishman they had to wait until Mr Holtby appeared for his evening meal. He was equally eager to see them, for he had heard that they were the only eye-witnesses. 'It's a mercy you weren't killed,' he said with feeling.

'How is he, sir?' asked William.

'Molony's all right. He's tough. The surgeon's saved his leg.'

'Thank God!' said Caroline.

'He won't be fit for heavy work for some time. He's a good lad, but he was very careless today. Those men should never have got near the tunnel – nor should you two, for that matter! But we'll say no more about that. There's a whole family in Ireland that depends on the money young Molony sends them. I'll keep him on if I possibly can.'

The next morning William and Peter went with him to the scene of the explosion. A gang was already busy clearing the site. All the powder barrels had been blown to smithereens. There would be a short delay until fresh supplies arrived. Meanwhile there were tons of fallen rock to be shifted and dangerous places made safe before the tunnel could be extended further into the hill.

'I don't suppose Sir Sefton imagined that he could hold up our progress for long,' said the engineer. 'He just wanted to show the world he was a dangerous man to cross. Vanity. We shall see.'

He was in no mood to let the outrage go unpunished. But after a day or two's consideration he began to admit that it might be better to take no action.

'We can't prove that he himself was involved. Can we even prove the identity of those two men?'

'*I'd* swear to them – in a court of law,' William assured him. But as he spoke the bold words he did not look forward to the experience. His father, he realized, would not be best pleased at his son getting mixed up in this conflict with an important man like Sir Sefton Creevey.

'But Caroline had never seen them before. Though I suppose she could identify them in court?'

That, however, suggested another uncomfortable thought. If Caroline was called to give evidence she could not avoid revealing her real name. If that got into the newspapers it would almost certainly come to Uncle Daniel's notice.

105

Mike Molony's evidence might not count for much. He had seen the men only at a distance. After that, what with his headlong descent into the cutting and his frantic efforts to stamp out the gunpowder train, his eyes had been occupied elsewhere.

Any thought of a successful prosecution faded some days later. Sir Sefton made it known throughout the neighbourhood that the suspected men had been miles away on the date in question. If there was any more gossip against them he was prepared personally to testify to their alibi.

'These magistrates hang together,' said Mr Holtby in disgust. 'They won't want to call another Justice of the Peace a liar. I've talked the matter over with my directors. They think it's wiser to take no action.'

William was equally disgusted, but he saw that the rest of his family were relieved. So officially the Cragdale Heights explosion remained an unsolved mystery, though few people in Redford doubted who had been behind it.

Mike Molony's injury was slow to heal. He could not put much weight on his damaged leg. He was unable to use pick and shovel or manoeuvre the huge wheelbarrows with their heavy loads. At William's suggestion Mr Thornton offered him temporary work in the stables.

'Can you work with horses, lad?'

Mike grinned. 'Did ye iver know an Irishman who couldn't, sor?'

Fred of course found points to criticize, but with everybody else at the inn the boy soon became a favourite. Caroline took a special interest in his recovery.

'I hope you've set your mother's mind at rest?'

He stared. 'She'll not know, please God.'

It was her turn to stare. 'But surely – I thought you must be so close? That awful day, when you were in such pain, you were calling out for her. Like a child.' She bit her lip, afraid she had embarrassed him. But he grinned back cheerfully as light dawned.

'Nay, Miss Caroline, it was the Holy Mother o' God I was callin' on. The pain was cruel. Sure, I thought me number was up! I thought I was dyin', so I did.'

Their laughter removed the brief embarrassment. 'But surely,' she said, 'you have told her, since?'

He looked awkward. 'I'm no hand wi' the pen.'

She should have thought of that. So many of her father's parishioners had been illiterate. 'Could *I* help?' she asked. 'If you told me what you'd like me to write – "

'She'd not be able to read it,' he said miserably.

No one in his family could read or write. They lived in Connemara on the far tip of the west coast. Hardly anyone in the village could read.

She would not give up. Again she thought back to her own father. 'You have a church? A clergyman – a priest, you'd call him?'

'Sure, there's old Father O'Donnell – '

'Then I'll write through him,' she said firmly. 'Your poor mother ought to have word of you now and again.'

'Ye're an angel,' he said.

And no doubt, she thought, *you* could be a bit of a devil, but she did not say so.

Fred did not welcome her interest in Mike's welfare.

107

He scowled when he came into the stables and found her reading to him the answer she had received from the village priest.

'I'm only interrupting Mike for a moment,' she explained hastily. 'It's my only chance to catch him. Maids aren't supposed to go anywhere near the men's quarters.'

'I should hope *not*,' said Fred severely. Grooms and stable-lads slept in the lofts above the horses' stalls.

'But Aunt Matty was all in favour of my helping him.'

'She would be! So long as you don't waste his time. But with all these coaches, and the mails going in and out so punctually, the stables have to work to the clock.'

'So do we in the house!' she assured him tartly. 'I try to catch Mike at the right moment — but I have to find the right moment myself, too.'

Fred snorted and marched out. He'd dearly love to rearrange their duties, she thought, so that her own free moments never coincided with Mike's.

Fred, she had realized from the start, was the one fly in the ointment of her happy existence here. He was absurdly jealous of William, his 'kid brother' as he liked to call him. Now he was even more absurdly jealous of Mike Molony, who could not be dismissed as anyone's kid brother.

Mike towered above almost everyone. The gentlest tap from his bunched fist would have stretched Fred on the stable straw. Only you didn't do that to your employer's son. And Mike wouldn't want to do it to anyone. He was like a massive good-natured coach horse as he lumbered round the yard, his iron-shod boots themselves sounding like hooves.

At her next encounter with Mike he whispered: 'He says if I need another letter wrote, not to trouble you or take you off your work. *He'll* write it for me.' He made a face. 'Won't sound the same though.'

'Take no notice,' she said defiantly. 'We've a perfect right.' But she knew that for Mike's sake she must be careful, or Fred would make his position at the inn impossible. Fred's jealousy was insane. She liked the Irish boy, she was sorry for him, but that was all. Their minds had no real meeting-place as hers had with William's, but never would with Fred's, if he was the last person in the world.

Fred, though, was becoming a trial. She could not avoid him at the Thorntons' family meals. And being 'family' he had the free run of the whole inn. She might meet him on the back stairs or he might appear suddenly in some guest-room she was dusting. Fred had a discreet footstep, very different from Mike's.

She was confident enough in one way. She could hold her own against this tiresome young man, but how could she stop the situation from becoming intolerable? He was the son of the house and the Thorntons had been so good to her. How could she stay under their roof if it came to open war with Fred? 'But I *won't* let myself be driven away,' she murmured to herself angrily. Tears pricked her eyes. It was unthinkable. She had won the independence she wanted, she was working well and giving satisfaction.

Things came to a climax she could not avoid. It was a sleepy afternoon, the great kitchen tidy and for once deserted. She was contentedly polishing some silver dish-covers. She never heard his stealthy entrance, only felt his hands stealing round under her arms, and then his hot breath on her cheek.

She spun round on her stool and stuffed the cleaning rag into his eager mouth.

He choked. 'You little bitch!'

'Think yourself lucky it wasn't *this*!'

She threatened him with the dish-cover in her other hand.

'You asked for that!' It was William's voice from the doorway. He was home unusually early from the work site.

'You keep out of this – *kid*!' Fred's sneer was withering.

'Then you leave Caroline alone. And apologize to her.'

'*Me* apologise? To a slut who goes with stable-boys!'

That was when William lashed out. He admitted to Caroline afterwards that he had been very lucky to catch his brother off balance. Never in his life before had he managed to knock Fred down, though he had often wanted to.

Fred fell with a most satisfying crash. Surveying him on the stone-slabbed floor Caroline could not help crying out in triumph: 'You don't know how *silly* you look!'

But Fred's expression was murderous as he struggled to his feet. It was fortunate that just then his mother's cool voice rang out: 'I thought you boys had outgrown this kind of thing years ago! In front of Caroline too!'

A good thing, thought the girl, she doesn't know it was all because of Caroline.

All three young people stood looking rather sheepish. Even Mrs Thornton herself was, for once, at a loss to know how best to end the awkward situation. Suddenly she seemed to have an inspiration. Looking very straight at Fred she said quietly: 'You had better come to my room, Frederick. You were asking me earlier for some writing paper. I will give you some.'

If that was for writing a letter on Mike's behalf it did not seem a good moment to argue the point.

14

For several days William was conscious of an ominous atmosphere.

Elder brothers did not like to be beaten. Younger brothers had to get used to it. 'I never had a brother, older or younger, or a sister,' said Caroline ruefully, 'so I don't know.'

William did. Fred would not forget that humiliation, with Caroline laughing at him down on the floor. He would find some way to get his revenge. But how? And how soon?

At least he had left off pestering the girl. He had called her a 'slut'. He must realize that he had lost any chance in that quarter. For himself, William was not afraid. He might not be so lucky again, if they came to blows, but Fred would think twice about that.

Fred had not apparently made any further trouble with the Irish boy. He had not after all repeated his offer to write Mike's letters for him. Caroline would be free to do so, but she would not trespass on Fred's domain by entering the stables.

William shrugged his shoulders and concentrated on his duties for Mr Holtby.

The tunnel was advancing steadily through the rocky wall of Cragdale Heights. Sir Sefton had made no further attempt to hinder the work. He seemed to have accepted the situation — and, through his lawyers, the company's compensation money for the right to carry the line across the valley. Holtby could now send his men over the ridge to begin excavation of the tunnel from the other end. He took care, though, always to keep a group of burly navvies there to protect the work.

Soon the onset of winter weather would hamper work on the open moors. Tunnelling would continue, but otherwise Holtby would turn his attention to easier stretches of the route, paying only occasional visits to Redford to check progress. William faced the glum prospect of being at Fred's beck and call again. Caroline seemed relieved that he was not yet being offered an apprenticeship and taken away from home.

Four days passed without incident after that scene in the kitchen. On the fifth afternoon he came down early from the work site. Holtby had an urgent letter to catch the evening mail for London.

Swinging down the hill into the outskirts of the town he heard the furious drumming of hooves on the Cragdale road below. Probably a post-chaise, he thought. Enough noise for a four-horse team. Chaises could come spanking along at a gallop, whereas coach horses kept to a steady trot. That was why chaises were expensive to hire and used mainly by well-to-do people who did not mind paying for the privacy and extra speed of a light vehicle they need not share with strangers. Chaises were specially welcome at the inns. The travellers expected splendid meals and wines, served in a private room. Prices were increased accordingly. So were everybody's tips.

William reached the main road just as the chaise flashed by. There was no driver, of course, just a postilion riding as usual the nearside leader. A single bulky passenger filled the space designed for two or three. The carriage shot down the High Street, contemptuous of other traffic and passers-by. As he expected and hoped, it wheeled skilfully into the yard of the Coach and Horses.

By the time William had handed in Holtby's letter to the postmaster the passenger had vanished into the inn, the postilion had dismounted, and Fred was taking his instructions for four fresh horses.

'Not sure when he's starting back. He'll say when.' The postilion was a dapper little man, rather grand in his shiny white hat, his white cord breeches and short blue jacket, his pearl-buttoned yellow waistcoat and the spotless white stock knotted under his chin. 'Gather it's urgent business — must be, if he's going back tonight. Doesn't do to ask, though.'

'Certainly not,' said Fred.

William wondered if it could be railway business. One of Holtby's directors from the Lancashire side? He hoped he would not have to go flying back to the work site to fetch the engineer. If so, Fred must let him have a pony.

He went indoors and walked straight into Caroline. They had barely exchanged a word when they were interrupted by Amy. 'Your auntie wants you! In the drawing-room. Quick.' It sounded urgent. Caroline shot off obediently.

William followed a minute or two later, not dreaming

that he was concerned. As he passed through to the family's private quarters he heard a thunderous voice from the open doorway ahead.

'A fine dance you've led us all this time, you little baggage! Driving your poor auntie nearly frantic!'

With cold horror he realized that the 'auntie' referred to was not his mother. All became plain when Caroline answered, shakily but with spirit: 'I'm sorry, Uncle Daniel. I didn't mean to. But I considered I had a perfect right – '

'Right? A child of your age *has* no rights!'

'I am not a child!'

'In law you are. And I must remind Mr Thornton here – *and* his wife – they've put themselves in a decidedly awkward position. Harbouring you like this – '

'Harbouring?' William's mother sounded scandalized. 'You make it sound as if we had done something dreadful. Caroline came to me for shelter. I was her mother's oldest friend – '

'Perhaps. But you are not a relative. You have no standing. So now I am taking her back, as I have every right to do. This minute.'

'*No!*' shrieked Caroline.

William took an impetuous step forward but managed to check himself before rushing into the room. If his father saw him he might be sent away and the door closed against him. Then he would hear no more. That would be intolerable.

Caroline's best hope lay with his parents. If anyone could handle this appalling Uncle Daniel they would. His father was speaking now in that quiet, reasonable tone that had calmed so many storms. In his time, he used to say, he had dealt with all sorts, from a drunken duke downwards.

'But would you not consider for a moment, Mr Snaith, there is more in this than a strict point of law? Caroline is also a human being. She has been happy with us – '

'Oh, I *have!*' agreed Caroline fervently.

'If you would allow her to stay, sir – for the present?'

'Not for a moment longer! I had plans for this girl – her aunt and I had great plans. She had prospects, which she may now have ruined.'

'She has prospects here, modest at least,' said William's mother with dignity. 'We are giving her a good training, she is intelligent, a fast learner – '

'Prospects? Oh, in the innkeeping trade, you mean?' Mr Snaith's tone was scathing. 'That's hardly what I had in mind for her. I was thinking of marriage, a *good* marriage, into the gentry. God knows if this crazy escapade won't have put paid to all thought of that. How can we check the gossip? Once it's whispered that she's spent all this time at an *inn*? Working!'

William had never heard his father so near to losing his temper. 'This is a respectable establishment, sir. One of the best-known in Yorkshire. Let me tell you, sir – '

'And let me tell *you*, sir, if you try to hold my niece here I'll make your name a byword throughout the North of England. Pack your bag, miss. And you, Mrs Thornton, kindly see that my niece is down in ten minutes. We have a long drive before us. We may have to break our journey, but we shall certainly not stay under *this* roof.'

William stepped back as his mother brushed past him with Caroline. They were both in tears. His mother was saying in a choked voice: 'It's the law, my dear, we can't *do* anything.'

He knew she was right. Mr Snaith had the law on his side. The Thorntons could not stand against him.

The two men continued talking icily. Pressing home his victory Mr Snaith said maliciously: 'I think, while I wait, I will take a glass of your best madeira.'

Now it was William's father who had a choke in his voice. 'If you wish, sir.'

'You are bound to serve me,' said the millowner triumphantly, 'this being a public inn!'

'To serve you, yes. But not to take your money.' When the wine was brought, Mr Thornton ignored the offered coin.

They went down into the yard. Mike was helping Fred to harness the new team. Though postilions usually changed after every stage the same man was riding back for the start of the return journey. Word had got round. Sympathetic maids and stable-hands were watching from a discreet distance.

Caroline came out, cloaked and bonneted, pale, her eyes misty. They met William's. It was too public a moment for proper goodbyes, they could only whisper a few words. She glanced towards Fred, tightening a harness strap. 'Say goodbye to Frederick for me.'

Her uncle caught the name. He marched across. 'So *you're* "F. Thornton"?' he said in a positively genial tone. Fred looked suddenly shifty and embarrassed.

'Yes, sir,' he mumbled.

'I'm glad someone in this family has a sense of responsibility!'

Mr Snaith clambered ponderously into the chaise.
Caroline shrank away on the seat as far as possible. Fred
slammed the door. The postilion urged his own mount
forward and the team responded. The chaise wheeled out
into the street.

William saw everything clear now. His fists clenched
instinctively but he had to control himself somehow. He
glared into his brother's face with hatred.

'It was *you*, was it?'

15

'You are not a prisoner.' Uncle Daniel paused in his breakfast routine of opening letters and forced his features into what was meant to be a kindly expression.

Caroline bowed her head but answered neither yes nor no. She felt as much a prisoner as if she were fettered in a dungeon.

She was free, certainly, to walk in and out of the house, merely expected to mention what reason was taking her into the town. But real freedom? She could not possibly run back to the Thorntons, where Uncle Daniel would instantly look for her. That family had done so much for her, but she must not make trouble for them. On the long drive back to Eldonby her uncle had left her in no doubt about what trouble he had the power to make. An innkeeper depended on the patronage of the good-class law-abiding public. A dispute with a man in Uncle Daniel's position, a legal case that might be reported in the newspapers, could ruin his business.

The road back to Redford was barred to her. She had nowhere else to go. For the moment she must submit.

Aunt Louisa was surprisingly forgiving. Though she would utter no criticism of her husband she was cautiously sympathetic. When Uncle Daniel was safely absent at mill or mine or magistrates' court she even allowed herself a guilty interest in Caroline's life at the Coach and Horses. She remembered her sister's friendship with Mrs Thornton and could not hide her envy. When Caroline warmed to her interest and gave vivid descriptions of the servants and guests, her aunt even began to reveal a sense of humour. But when Uncle Daniel strode back into the house she closed up like a daisy at nightfall.

'Of course, you can't possibly go back to school, my dear.'

Her uncle, she said, was firm on that. The other girls would question her and worm out the facts behind her long absence. That must not happen.

Caroline did not mind about school – she felt she had outgrown it – but she resented the way she was prevented from resuming such slight friendships as she had made there.

'You will be making new friends,' Aunt Louisa promised. 'Your uncle's going to spare nothing. He's going to make a lady of you.'

New dresses, a drawing master to come to the house, music lessons till she could dumbfound visitors with her piano-playing, deportment, even Italian. To dabble in that language was apparently a suitable accomplishment for a well-bred girl. She need not actually visit those outlandish parts.

'These are the necessary ingredients,' said Aunt Louisa, 'for the making of a young lady.'

Ingredients, thought Caroline rebelliously, I am not a cake! She did not want to be mixed, thrust into an oven and baked. The thought of ovens took her back to Mrs Thornton's kitchen with its warmth and delectable smells, the chatter and clatter and jollity of the maids.

One morning Uncle Daniel looked up fiercely from his letters. 'Hadn't the Thorntons another boy? Was his name William?'

Her heart almost stopped. 'Yes, uncle. Is that letter – '

'Yes! He has had the impertinence to write to you.'

Her hand flashed across like a bird. He ignored it. He tore the paper across and across into small pieces. 'Emily,' he told the maid, 'take these and put them in the kitchen stove.'

But half an hour later Emily brought her the workbox she had not asked for. 'I just thought you might want it, miss,' she said with a meaning smile. 'Could cost me my place,' she whispered.

Caroline raised the lid and saw the torn scraps of paper. 'It shan't, Emily,' she promised.

By next day she felt able to compose a suitable reply. She assured William that she was well, not unduly cast down but furious. She went on: *'So you see that you cannot write to me here. But this maid tells me she has a married sister who keeps a little lodging-house in the town. Mail arrives for various names, so nobody would think it odd. Emily's sister says we may use this arrangement so long as we keep it secret.'* Nobody must be in danger of Uncle Daniel's wrath. As for telling his own parents, William must do as he thought fit. But it would be very sad, she could not help hinting, if they felt it was their duty to interfere.

William's eagerly-awaited response was slipped, untorn, into her workbox a few days later. He agreed that they should take no unnecessary risks.

Aunt Louisa, though knowing nothing of this, did

exhort Caroline earnestly: 'We must try not to vex your uncle, my dear. He has a great deal on his mind just now.'

She was aware of that. A strike was threatened at his colliery, where, like other mine-owners, he had cut the weekly wage to half a crown. Two months' toil underground, she thought, to earn one pound – no wonder the men were rebellious! She remembered the pay the navvies were getting to dig Mr Holtby's tunnel. At Redford the railway project had brought more prosperity all round. Here at Eldonby she realized how different things were in other parts of the country.

Uncle Daniel had further worries too. Officials had been going round the mines and cotton-mills, poking their noses into matters that did not concern them, asking questions and scribbling down answers in their notebooks. A report was to be made to Parliament about the working hours and conditions of small children. Uncle Daniel did not like the sound of that. 'I'm only doing the same as everyone else does,' he grumbled.

He could no longer forbid all mention of the Chartists – there were too many about, even in Eldonby, busy-body agitators demanding that every grown man, rich or poor, should have a vote. 'A fine thing!' he sneered. Secretly Caroline thought it might be. But why not women? Even the Chartists said nothing about women. They wanted this Charter only for themselves. They were all signing a petition to Parliament.

To hear Uncle Daniel you would have thought the nation was boiling up to a terrible revolution like the one in France fifty years ago. It would fall to him, as a magistrate, to see that law and order were kept in Eldonby.

'It's only two years,' he said, 'since that disgraceful affair at Newport. We don't want that sort of thing here.'

Aunt Louisa shuddered. 'Surely it couldn't happen in Eldonby?'

'Don't be too sure. There's been mills burnt down in Lancashire this year.'

Hundreds of special constables were being sworn in, good solid fellows with a stake in the country, Uncle Daniel called them, farmers and shopkeepers and suchlike. 'But we may need more than that, come May,' he said darkly.

'Why May, my dear?'

He answered patiently, not expecting a mere female to know anything about it. 'Because in May they're going to present their wonderful petition to Parliament. And if it's rejected, as it's sure to be, that's when the real trouble will start. More, maybe, than special constables can cope with.'

He was triumphant when it was announced, a month or two later, that a regiment of light cavalry was to be billeted in the town. 'Just the thing! Hussars! A charge with sabres – then we'll see those fellows run!'

He claimed credit for himself that they were being sent to Eldonby. Caroline could believe him. He was becoming important in the neighbourhood. His stern severity on the bench had won him a reputation. And at a time like this magistrates played a vital part. Even the troops had to have their authority before they could use force.

'If the situation demands it,' Uncle Daniel explained, rolling out the words with relish, 'the Justices of the Peace will read the Riot Act. Only after that may the troops open fire.'

'Fire?' said Aunt Louisa in horror. 'Oh, dear — '

'A few volleys would be enough,' he assured her, 'but a cavalry charge would be even better.'

He can hardly wait, thought Caroline disgustedly. He would read this Riot Act as pompously as he read the Lesson in church on Sundays.

The coming of the Hussars gave him another cause for satisfaction. 'I thought, Louisa, it would be very proper if we showed our appreciation with a party for the officers.'

'Here? In this house?' She was flabbergasted.

'Why not? It's big enough.'

Alarm gave her courage. 'But don't you think we should consider — '

'I've already spoken with the colonel. He has accepted.'

Aunt Louisa was silenced.

Whatever his knowledge of military matters Caroline had to admit that in social manoeuvres he was a master of strategy. He had stolen a march on his rivals. Given time to think, several local families — titled, some of them — would have been more obvious people to entertain the officers. Daniel Snaith would have seemed to be pushing himself forward absurdly. But his position as magistrate had given him a natural contact with the colonel. He had got his blow in first. The invitation had been accepted. Who now could question his right to give the party?

And who would want to miss it, thought Caroline,

suppressing her inner laughter at his cunning. Those who looked down upon the jumped-up Mr Snaith, and would normally have declined any invitation to his house, could hardly do so in this case. There could be only one such welcoming party for the gallant Hussars. Not to be there might suggest sympathy with the Chartists.

Everybody who *was* anybody would be there. If any gentleman was stubborn enough to hesitate, his wife and daughters would persuade him. Having once accepted a Snaith invitation they would be unable to ignore others in the future. Good manners would dictate that this one be returned. By once crossing the Snaith threshold they would have placed Uncle Daniel for ever within the magic circle of the somebodies.

Caroline saw that it would be worth every penny of the appalling expense – the champagne, the hired flunkeys, the musicians brought from Manchester. Being young and normal, she began to look forward to it herself.

She was to be included in the lavish investment. 'A real ball dress,' Uncle Daniel instructed Aunt Louisa. 'Get her what's proper. Nothing cheap. Nothing dowdy,' he added with foresight, for which Caroline was thankful, knowing her aunt's unadventurous taste. A week later she wrote to William:

'*He took us with him to Manchester – he had business on the Cotton Exchange, but made time to take us to the best shops . . . My very first ball dress! A kind of primrose colour, that tones with my hair . . . Shot silk –* ' she allowed for a boy's possible ignorance ' *– which means the colour changes as I move. Cut very low, off the shoulder, so I hope it will not be a cold evening. Flounced skirt,* very full, VERY grand! Flowers on the shoulders and — ' She stopped. She could not write the word *'breast'* in a letter to William. Oh well, there were flowers also on that wonderful skirt. She finished the sentence, *'skirt'*.

The great day came. So, to judge from the flow of fine carriages, did all the best families. So did the officers, breathtaking creatures in exotic dress uniform, like long-legged water birds in their tight tapering blue trousers with gold stripes. When they danced they became birds of paradise, their scarlet Turkish-style dolmans swinging casually from one shoulder, the empty sleeve whirling wildly in the rhythm of the waltz.

The girls of Eldonby were swept off their feet, both literally and metaphorically, Caroline among them. For the moment her opinion of her uncle mellowed.

There were not enough officers to go round but he had made sure there would be plenty of other young gentlemen to make up for it. He had warned her jokingly — his jokes were apt to be heavy — not to lose her heart to a soldier. She guessed it was no part of his scheme that she should. His eye was on the upper class of his own Lancashire.

Tonight, as niece of the host and hostess, Caroline had no need to fear lack of partners. After two hours of incessant quadrilles and lancers and whirlwind waltzes she was thankful when the musicians laid down their instruments and trooped off for refreshment. Her last partner, a Hussar lieutenant, offered to bring her an ice and they moved thankfully into the cool quiet of the orangery.

It was a modest structure leading out to the garden, but still quite a novelty in the neighbourhood. Tiny trees stood in their tubs, sheltered from the cold Lancashire winds. In another month or two their white blossoms would turn into tiny oranges, ornamental but inedible. The small windowpanes reflected the lights of a hundred candles. Other guests were standing or strolling about. It was hardly private but, as the Hussar said thankfully, at least conversation was possible.

He looked intelligent, she thought. But Uncle Daniel, who seemed to be everywhere, had seen them and came sailing across.

'Ah, there you are, my dear! You must not neglect our other guests.' To soften the hint he said to the officer: 'Splendid to have you young fellows in Eldonby!'

'Everyone is most kind, sir. We only wish the reason for our being here was happier.'

'Happier?' Uncle Daniel's eyebrows shot up. 'Couldn't be happier! We're so thankful to have your protection against those ruffians. We shan't have our houses burnt over our heads.'

'I don't think it will come to anything like that, sir. The poor people are obviously suffering greatly, but I can't imagine they'll resort to violence. We'd be very sorry if we had to fire a shot.'

'*Sorry?* Why do you think you've been sent to us? We expect you to teach the rabble a lesson.'

'We shall keep the peace, sir, of course.' Caroline could have hugged herself as the courteous young officer stood up to her uncle. 'But no British soldier would wish to

127

shoot down his own countrymen. These folk have just grievances – '

Uncle Daniel looked liable to burst. 'Dammit, young man, you talk like a Chartist yourself. Mind you don't find yourself facing a court martial.'

'I'm not alone in my feelings, sir,' said the Hussar quietly. 'A year or two ago I was attached to Sir Charles Napier's headquarters at Nottingham. I heard him say, the people should have the vote, it's their right.'

'And him a general! Scandalous!'

Just then the musicians struck up again, which gave an excuse to break off the awkward conversation. Braving her uncle's obvious disapproval, Caroline accepted the officer's extended hand and walked back with him to the dance-floor.

That was April. In the next few weeks the situation grew uglier. A mill was burnt down at Manchester. There were strikes, with non-strikers thrown into the canals. There were rumours of men collecting arms and manufacturing their own pikes and hand-grenades. There was talk of secret drilling on the moors. The official report on child labour in mills and mines that Uncle Daniel was dreading was published and horrified the country. It horrified Uncle Daniel too. His profits were threatened.

The Chartist petition was presented to Parliament – and rejected. And people spoke now of an armed march on Buckingham Palace to dethrone the young queen.

16

It was some time before William grasped the seriousness of the situation developing throughout the country.

Redford had neither mines nor mills, few workless people, no prominent Chartist agitators. The railway absorbed him. With the coming of spring Holtby had resumed full-scale operations on the uplands. A snake of iron rails was creeping along the causeway over the bog. The two ends of the tunnel had met with uncanny accuracy. Now came the next challenge — the viaduct with its tall arches soaring up from the valley-floor and the bridge spanning the central gap above the river.

It was a time that William was never to forget, exhausting to the body but exhilarating to the mind. Peter Spaxton was near the end of his apprenticeship. He would remain on the site as a qualified assistant engineer. Holtby would be taking on a new apprentice. It was most likely that William would be offered his chance.

Everything would have been splendid, if only Caroline had still been there. That gap not even Holtby's engineering magic could fill. Letter-writing helped a little — the girl wrote wonderful letters which he could not match. He was handier with figures than with phrases.

Life sounded grim in Eldonby. That impression was confirmed by Waterloo Walter, who slept there at the

Lancashire end of his run. He had not seen Caroline but he could fill in the background she merely hinted at.

'That uncle o' hers is the most hated man in the town,' he told William. 'I don't wonder he makes a fuss o' the soldiers – he'll need 'em if folk are tried too far.'

It was a relief to chat with Walter on his alternate evenings at the Coach and Horses. With Mike Molony also William could talk about Caroline, for the young Irishman missed her too. With his parents William had to be careful. When they referred to her, with affection and concern, he felt it best to say nothing about the secret correspondence. As for Fred, they were nowadays scarcely on speaking terms.

The coachman's reports on Eldonby made him more anxious for Caroline. But he now realized that the fear of violence was spreading generally. Redford was quiet enough but you could not live in a busy coaching inn without picking up rumours from all quarters. He overheard them in the coffee-room. He saw them in discarded newspapers from distant towns.

Holtby came back from one of his flying visits to London with grim news. The government was definitely bracing itself for disorder, even an armed rising. As a former soldier Holtby was sure that the troops could be relied upon and would crush any such attempt. But at a cost.

'There seems to be discontent everywhere. But it sounds especially bad in Lancashire.' He seldom spoke of Caroline, though like everyone at the inn he had heard of her dramatic departure. William sometimes wondered if Holtby was not more aware of his friendship with the girl than he revealed. Now the engineer mentioned her. 'Our beautiful Caroline,' he said. 'If that detestable uncle of hers had any true concern for her welfare he'd send her back here till all this has blown over.'

'He'd never do that.' William hesitated, then added: 'You don't think she'd be in any danger, sir?'

'She'd be safer here. Anyone *can* get hurt in a time of civil disorder.'

'They've got these Hussars stationed in the town.' It suddenly occurred to William that this might not be a good sign. Perhaps it indicated Eldonby as a likely trouble-spot.

'Ye-es. Mr Snaith seems such an unpopular figure . . .'

'But no one could have anything against her!'

'No. I'm sure you've no need to worry on her account.'

Holtby did not sound quite sure. Only sure that he wanted to drop the subject and was sorry he had started it. Sensing his reluctance, William did not like to say more.

Her next letter did nothing to cheer him. Life at Uncle Daniel's was more than ever like being in prison. The ball for the officers had been a mere interlude in her dreary existence.

'*He does not like me to go out alone,*' she wrote. '*So, as I have no friends of my own age, it must be with Aunt Louisa in the carriage, because of her bad feet. The only exercise I can take is along the canal towpath on the other side of our orchard wall. How I sigh for the moors round Redford! I shall never forget that day you took me up to see the tunnel.*'

Nor shall I, he thought. He read on:

'Even for a stroll along the canal I am not supposed to go alone. The gardener's boy must escort me. My uncle insists that he keeps ten paces behind me, though the path is wide enough for us both. He says it is to "discourage familiarity" — but it does not add to my enjoyment! It is better when Emily can be spared from her other duties. She and I can walk side by side, talk and sometimes even giggle if we have secrets to share. Like this correspondence, which only her kindness makes possible.'

Her uncle could not see why she should be bored. Hadn't she her needlework, and the pianoforte, and the books she set so much store by?

'Thank God for the circulating library!' she wrote with feeling. There was nothing to read in the house. Her uncle never opened anything but an account-book. Her aunt admitted innocently that she had 'never properly finished the Bible'. The circulating library had the latest novels, like The Old Curiosity Shop. But Uncle Daniel could not see why she need go there herself. Surely one of the servants could return books and fetch others? 'He can't understand,' she wrote, 'that one must CHOOSE. Every book is different from every other book in the whole WORLD.'

A week later she struck a more ominous note. 'It is like living in a besieged castle. Since the attempt to burn down one of his mills he has taken to carrying a loaded pistol! I tell him he is like an old-time highwayman, but he says there is nothing amusing about it, and secretly I think he is right. I am getting frightened myself. When I see threats and insults daubed on our own gateposts I get very frightened indeed.'

So did William when he read that. It did not sound like the Caroline he knew.

He asked Walter how things were looking at Eldonby.

'Ugly,' said the old coachman. 'Very ugly.'

'But surely, if it comes to fighting, the soldiers – '

'Nay, it'll not come to fightin', not while the soldiers are there.'

'Then she's in no real danger, surely?'

'She could be in worse danger,' said Walter.

'*Worse?*'

'I've heard whispers, lately, sittin' over me evenin' pint, nobody thinkin' I was takin' in a word of it. Some are sayin', ye can't fight the Hussars, but why not strike at the mesters through their weak point? They've wives an' children. Take some as hostages. Then ye've summat to bargain with.'

William eyed him aghast. 'They'd kidnap them? A young girl like her?'

'Specially her! Her uncle bein' the best hated man around. I'll bet the notion's occurred to *him.* Why's he watchin' her more careful than ever? It's the Chartists he's afeard of, I reckon. I've heard no names mentioned, but I'd lay a guinea they *are* plannin' something o' that nature.'

William groaned. It seemed all too likely. But the coachman had no hard evidence that could be reported to anyone in authority. Uncle Daniel seemed to be taking general precautions. What more could be done without definite information?

There was only one other person he felt he could talk to. He sought out Mike Molony. The Irish boy listened in silence. Then he spoke.

'Know what *I'd* do – if she was *my* gal?'

133

'No. That's why I'm asking you.'

'If she was my gal,' said Mike slowly, 'I'd go over there an' get her out of it all. No matter what. No matter who.'

17

She had not expected another letter from William so soon. She was delighted to find one in her workbox.

His letters were usually rather stilted, not lively like his talk, a mere shadow of the real boy. But in her present circumstances they were particularly welcome, a reminder that elsewhere normal life went on.

This letter was different. No time wasted on polite inquiries in conventional phrases, conscientiously following adult instructions on the 'proper' way to write. It looked untidy, he was clearly scribbling away under pressure. But it was fluent and decisive, like an engineer (she thought, with a smile) setting down plans to deal with a problem. Only once did he say, '*if you agree*'. Otherwise he clearly assumed, step by step, that she would. There was no alternative. Time was vital.

He was worried by her last letter. (She must have allowed her mounting nervousness to show between the lines.) '*You're in danger where you are,*' he told her, '*but we're going to get you out of it.*' He did not say who '*we*' were. They avoided using names in their letters in case one fell into the wrong hands, but his next sentence showed that '*our Irish friend*' but his own family was not. *Nor need they be. She would be under their roof for only an hour or two before moving on. 'A kind gentleman — whom you know and*

135

will trust — has offered to arrange for you to stay with a married lady, his sister.'

Caroline flushed with excitement. How well he had worked everything out — and so quickly! The kind gentleman must be Holtby. She remembered that he had a married sister in London. William's plan was as well worked out as a stage-coach timetable.

He would come over with Mike on the Twin Roses coach next Tuesday. They would go to the lodging-house kept by Emily's sister. If Caroline had any last-minute difficulty she must send word there. Otherwise, they would follow — in reverse — the route she had described to him after her original escape. They would walk along the canal to the back gate of her uncle's property, then through his orchard and over the gardens to the door of the orangery. She must wait inside, hiding, until they arrived. As near three o'clock as possible.

It was well thought out. They should be clear of the house long before the maids were stirring and have ample time for a leisurely breakfast at the Lamb and Flag before taking their seats on the coach. She sparkled at the very thought. No awkwardness this time! She would be meeting Waterloo Walter and Gentleman Joe as old friends — and she would have her travelling companions. Even if word got back to Uncle Daniel it would be too late by then to matter. She would be in London. She remembered those early evening coaches to London. She would have only long enough in Redford for a joyful reunion with William's parents — or they could turn a blind eye to her presence if they thought it wiser.

William, however, seemed to have provided for everything. Uncle Daniel would probably not check on the coach passengers or imagine that she had gone to Redford, for William was planning to make her disappearance look like a Chartist kidnapping. Her uncle would be searching in all the wrong directions while she was vanishing into the nameless multitudes of London.

Really, she thought, William was *rather* clever. Within an hour or two she had written her reply agreeing to his plan and the co-operative Emily was slipping to the post office.

Joy had replaced her mounting depression and anxiety. She looked forward impatiently to next Tuesday night.

Meanwhile William's complicated preparations went well.

Holtby asked no questions and held aloof, yet had a knack of facilitating the arrangements. A separate gang of workmen were busy on a preparatory job at a point far west of Redford where the railway would pass quite close to the coach-road. He suddenly discovered the need for an errand which William could perform, taking urgent instructions to the foreman along with a bag of money for the men's wages. It was best that he should not travel alone in such unsettled times, so Mr Thornton willingly released Mike to go with him. It meant travelling out by the Twin Roses on Tuesday morning, lodging somewhere overnight, and returning by the coach the following afternoon.

It all went smoothly. The foreman met them at the midday stop. They then remounted the coach and went right on to Eldonby, where they sought out the lodging-house kept by Emily's sister. Mrs Askew seemed to be expecting them and most conveniently had a bedroom vacant. Knowing that young gentlemen liked to keep late hours, she trustingly provided them with a door key. They paid their reckoning in advance, as they would be in a hurry to catch the coach early next morning.

After Mrs Askew's excellent supper they went out, officially to explore the town, actually to find the way to the Snaiths' house along the canal. The sun was setting, its blinding red reflected from the placid water. It was not hard to identify the boundary of Uncle Daniel's domain, a long stone wall eight feet high. The fruit trees peeped over the top. Recessed in the masonry, like a house door, was the gate by which Caroline had previously escaped and would now escape again. They were not surprised to find that it was locked.

'They'll be more careful now,' said William.

'We'll soon get over that. If it's only bolted, we'll slip the bolts once we're inside. If it's locked, and no key – '

'We can help her scramble over.'

'Sure, the girl won't let that stop her.'

They walked back into the town. There were soldiers about, but not in such numbers as they had expected. A man told them that half the troops had been called away to deal with some disturbance in another town ten miles away. They went back to the lodging-house but did not return Mrs Askew's key. She did not ask for it. They guessed that her young sister Emily had told her enough to make her sympathetic and discreet. She would have guessed anyhow that William was the writer of those letters that arrived for Caroline.

For the same reason, no doubt, if she was awakened by their stealthy departure in the middle of the night, she did not stir to challenge them. By then the splendours of the sunset had been replaced by a grey drizzle. It was as well that they had reconnoitred beforehand and could find the gate in the wall. As they expected, it did not yield to their push.

Mike stooped, bracing himself. 'Up on me shoulders!' William obeyed, steadying himself with the palms of his hands against the rough stone. The Irish youth rose carefully, inch by inch, to his full height. William found he could easily get his hands over the parapet. He swung his leg over, straddling it. He gripped with his knees, as though riding bareback, and taking a firm hold with one hand reached down with the other to help Mike. It was a tense moment. He must on no account let Mike's greater weight pull him off. But his friend needed very little assistance and came sailing up light as a leaping deer.

They dropped silently into the long wet grass beneath the apple trees. Lawns and shrubberies stretched away in front of them towards the dark mass of Uncle Daniel's pretentious mansion. The orangery was easy to make out with its long expanse of dimly gleaming glass.

'She should be waiting in there.' William barely breathed the words.

'Got the paper?'

'I wouldn't forget that.'

He tapped his pocket, felt its reassuring rustle. He

had taken great pains in wording it, he would not have forgotten to bring it, and now he must on no account forget to leave it in the orangery where it would be sure to catch someone's eye.

It was brief, pencilled in crudest print to disguise his handwriting, but it was the nearest he had ever come to creating a piece of imaginative literature. Mike had been full of admiration when it had been read to him.

> TO DANIEL SNAITH ESQ MP
> *Your niece is in a place of safety and no harm*
> *will come to her*
> PROVIDED
> *that you publish a solemn declaration*
> *in the newspaper acknowledging your*
> *error in opposing the PEOPLE'S CHARTER,*
> *and calling upon all good men to support it.*
> *Our other demands will be communicated to you*
> *and when you accede to them she will be*
> RELEASED UNHARMED
> LONG LIVE THE PEOPLE'S CHARTER!!!

There was no likelihood that Uncle Daniel would tamely submit to this sort of thing, but it would put him off the true scent while Caroline got safely to London. Then, as previously, she could write to Aunt Louisa and reassure her. Very likely, by then, Uncle Daniel would have his hands full dealing with the genuine activities of the local Chartists. Anyhow, the fright would have done him no harm.

140

Before going forward they checked the gate from the inside. It was not only bolted but also locked.

'Never mind,' said William. He was impatient.

'Will ye hang on, now?' With his free hand Mike held William back while he bent forward and picked up a fallen branch. There was a note of warning in his voice. The branch swished in the grass as he swept it to and fro. The sharp metallic snap that followed was almost like a pistol-shot in the silence. William was steadied by the Irish boy's restraining grip. 'Hush ye! They'd not hear it, this far away.'

They stood motionless for a long minute. No light appeared at any of the windows. Mike spoke again.

''Tis lucky we didn't step on that. These contraptions can smash a man's leg.' William leant forward gingerly and peered down into the gloom. As far as he could see the device that had gone off so noisily was like a huge rat-trap, with a powerful spring and teeth that would snap through flesh and bone. A spring-gun would have been even worse and louder, but their use in England was now forbidden. Mike knew all about such things from his childhood poaching in Connemara.

He led the way cautiously forward, William close at his back. Beyond the orchard stretched the lawns, dangerously exposed to any watching eye. But there were shrubberies to right and left, with winding paths, so that they could use the dense cover without stepping into it at the risk of further man-traps. They reached the steps rising to the terrace. William saw a moving glimmer inside the orangery. 'Good *girl!*' he whispered to himself thankfully.

The next whisper came from Caroline herself as the glass door swung out silently. 'Oh, thank *God*!' Her voice was muffled against his shoulder.

'Have you a bag?'

'Over there!'

He saw it among the little tubs of orange trees. He detached himself gently and tiptoed over to get it.

'The paper,' Mike reminded him. 'Don't be forgettin' the paper!'

He pulled it from his pocket and laid it on the tiled floor where no one could miss it. He weighted it with a shard of broken pot. As his fingers curled round the handle of the bag a voice spoke from the shadowy doorway leading into the house.

'Stand where you are! Or I'll blow you to blazes!'

18

William had heard that voice before. It was the voice of a man used to giving orders and having them obeyed.

It would have been crazy to disobey them now. He and Mike must be clear targets, silhouetted against the first pallor of the dawn. A backward glance showed the futility of a dash for freedom. A lantern was bobbing in the orchard. Two shadowy figures came racing across the lawn.

'Keep your hands up!' barked Uncle Daniel. 'Who are you?'

'Chartists!' William tried to sound defiant. He had not prepared for this face-to-face encounter. He could only stick to the pretence and hope that Uncle Daniel would not remember that day at Redford. He and Mike should have worn masks or blacked their faces.

The man stepped forward. His nightshirt was stuffed inside his trousers. He was holding a pistol all right. He snarled at Caroline: 'What are *you* doing here, at this time of night?'

William broke in before she could answer. How could they hide the fact that she had been leaving of her own free will? He must do his best. 'We were taking her as a hostage – for our cause,' he said. 'We've left you a message – there, on the floor.'

Uncle Daniel however kept his pistol trained upon him. There were footsteps on the terrace outside. A young man burst into the orangery panting. Another pistol glinted in the rays of a lantern held by a man behind him.

'Jacob's run for the soldiers,' the young man reported. 'They *are* Chartists, Dad?'

'They say so. Bring that lantern closer, Bradwell.' His tone changed. 'Ah! I fancied I'd seen these two before. Pick up that paper, Bob. Read me what it says.'

William squirmed inwardly to hear its phrases awkwardly delivered by Caroline's cousin. He could hardly bring himself to look at her. But he did so, willing her to keep silent. As yet she had not uttered a syllable. He hoped that she was biding her time and thinking hard, making up her own story.

Young Snaith finished reading. ' "Long live the people's Charter!" ' he concluded without enthusiasm.

'Balderdash!' said Uncle Daniel. 'Who would believe such rubbish?' Then he chuckled. 'But the courts will accept it as evidence. Which is all that matters. Take notice, Bradwell. You too, Bob. You may be asked to swear that you found this paper here, in the presence of the prisoners – '

'But, Dad – '

'Don't interrupt. This rigmarole is enough to put the young blackguards in jail for years – perhaps to transport them to Australia. Attempted kidnapping! On their own written confession!' He was exultant.

With horror William read his thoughts. That quick,

144

unscrupulous mind, which had brought the man such success in business, would turn this Chartist pretence to advantage. He had recognized William and must have grasped instantly that this was a plot to take his willing niece back to Redford. He would ignore that and accept the hostage story at its face value. An attempted kidnapping was a far more serious offence, especially if linked with the Chartists. Helping a girl leave home was probably not a criminal matter at all, probably no more than a civil dispute for lawyers to wrangle over.

Caroline was just as quick to guess his intentions. 'Uncle!' she cried in fury. 'You can't *do* this!'

'You'll see what I can do, miss, and what I can't do. I'll talk to you later. Go back to your room.'

'I shall tell the court the truth!'

'You will not be called to give evidence. Or you will be disregarded as a hysterical young female,' he jeered. 'This paper speaks for itself.'

Before they could wrangle further there was a rush of booted feet and half a dozen Hussars with drawn sabres rushed on to the terrace. An officer entered the orangery and swept Caroline a magnificent salute.

'Are you all right, Miss Snaith?'

'I am not Miss "Snaith" but I am quite all right, Mr Witney.' She smiled and obviously knew him. 'I'm afraid this is not as pleasant as the last time you were here.'

Uncle Daniel asserted himself. 'I want these two young fellows taken in charge. They admit to being Chartists. The tall one, I believe, is Irish – '

'And proud of it,' said Mike. 'Why would I not be?'

145

'They have broken into my premises – '

Caroline interrupted. 'That is not strictly true, and I call you all to witness. They're here at my invitation. *I* unlocked this door.'

'They're here with an unlawful purpose,' said Uncle Daniel. 'They must have climbed over my orchard wall. They had no right to be on my property – '

'At my invitation,' Caroline repeated. 'I don't need to remind *you*, Mr Witney, I am very much a member of Mr Snaith's household. Unwillingly!'

The officer looked uncomfortable. He swung round on William and Mike. 'Have you any weapons?'

'No, sir,' they said together.

He turned back to Uncle Daniel. 'I'm a little uncertain,' he said stiffly, 'whether these lads have committed any offence – '

'They were kidnapping my niece as a hostage for their infernal Chartist conspiracy. Read this demand note! What more evidence do you want?'

'A girl being kidnapped,' said Caroline, 'doesn't usually pack her bag and come down in the middle of the night – and unlock the door.' With a mocking echo of her uncle she said, pointing to the bag, 'What more evidence do you want?'

William might have felt sorry for the embarrassed officer if he had not been feeling so sorry for himself. The Hussar was struggling to find words.

'I – I feel, sir – isn't this rather more of a family dispute than a breach of public order? Not quite the sort of thing we were sent here to deal with.'

'Let me remind you I am a magistrate. I am telling you to take these two into custody. They are Chartists.'

'But it's not a crime, merely to *be* a Chartist – '

'I might have expected this!' burst out Uncle Daniel. 'I recall our first conversation in this house. You're no better than a Chartist yourself, sir. My niece was being abducted at dead of night – '

'She denies that. You are her legal guardian?'

'Of course!'

'Strictly speaking, no, Daniel.'

The fresh voice, somewhat quavery, came from a lady who now advanced into the lantern light and stopped short when confronted by so many male faces. She clutched her dressing-gown more tightly about her. Bedroom slippers peeped from beneath a voluminous nightdress. Without doubt, Aunt Louisa.

'Forgive my appearance,' she said. 'I did not mean to show myself, but I feel now I really must intervene. Mr Snaith is the kindest man in the world,' she assured the officer. 'He desires only Caroline's welfare. But I do not think that my poor sister, when she died, meant him to rule her life.' Uncle Daniel broke in angrily but she went on with remarkable determination. 'I know, my dear, you have tried to explain everything to me – marriage made us one, as man and wife, and the law says that the whole of a wife's property belongs to her husband. But nothing can make you my sister's sister.' Even Uncle Daniel seemed unable to contradict this. 'And that's who she *said* was to take care of Caroline,' Aunt Louisa concluded triumphantly.

William took heart from this unexpected development. He had previously imagined that Caroline's aunt was no more than a 'dear old thing', but completely under the thumb of her husband. He realized now that she might help to save the situation. True, his plan to spirit Caroline away had proved a fiasco, but Uncle Daniel's scheme to have them arrested as genuine Chartists was getting no support from the Hussar officer. He had despatched his men to search the grounds for other intruders, but he clearly did not expect them to find any. It was just an excuse to get them out of the way.

So the danger of prison was lifted. It was now just a question of legal guardianship. Would Aunt Louisa's new-found independence hold or would Uncle Daniel browbeat her into submission, as he must so often have done before?

Before the man could start to bluster again William seized his chance. 'I'm sorry, Mrs Snaith,' he said respectfully, 'for causing all this upset. My name is Thornton — '

She smiled at him. 'You must be William. Caroline has told me about you. And your parents' kindness.'

'They know nothing about this,' he said hurriedly. 'They wouldn't defy the law, never for one moment.'

'I know how happy she was with them. Happier than here, I'm afraid,' Aunt Louisa admitted sadly. 'We meant well — '

'I'd made proper arrangements — she'd have gone straight to a lady's house — it would have been absolutely respectable — '

If the Thorntons had possessed a coat-of-arms those

last two words would have been the motto below the shield.

Uncle Daniel now sailed in, all guns blazing. 'You ask us to believe your father would not defy the law? He has done!'

Caroline and her aunt broke out in protest, but he shouted them down. 'Don't tell me this whipper-snapper is twenty-one. Till he is, he's an infant in terms of the law – his father is responsible for his actions. I warned Thornton. Now I can take him to court, I can ruin his business, drag his name through the mud – '

'But how can you, Daniel, if I'd signified *my* approval?'

'You can't!' cried Caroline, scenting victory. 'You'd be the laughing stock of Lancashire!'

Once again the officer tried to withdraw from the conflict that was not his concern. But Aunt Louisa detained him. 'I am so sorry we have dragged you and your men out of your beds for nothing. You must have some breakfast before you go. Bob, dear, put away that dreadful pistol, it frightens me – the maids can't be still asleep after all this hubbub. Find Cook and give her instructions. And Emily must take a tray for Mr Witney into the breakfast-room. Coffee – everything – '

Uncle Daniel's face was a thunderstorm about to break. 'I want more than coffee,' he cried chokingly, and plunged into the house.

'I must put some clothes on,' said Aunt Louisa. She turned to Caroline. 'You have never been happy here. And this will not be a very happy house for some time to come. So – and I mean this, my dear – if you wish to leave it you may do so, with my full approval. William, may I ask, what *had* you planned?'

'I've seats booked on the Twin Roses coach, ma'am.'

'Then I suggest you catch it. It would save weeks of miserable wrangling — I so hate argument. I know my weakness, her uncle might wear me down, he's so clever, he knows so much *more* about everything than I do. But if she has already gone — '

They did not hesitate. It was best to go at once and take breakfast at the Lamb and Flag. Cousin Bob, surprisingly, insisted on escorting them and carrying Caroline's bag. 'Never seen much of each other, have we?' he said gruffly. 'Pity.'

He would get his mother to write at once to the Thorntons, confirming that Caroline had left with her consent. Then, if his father tried to bully Aunt Louisa into a change of mind, it would be too late. 'Dad's motto in business — he's told me a dozen times. "Get summat in writing." ' Bob chuckled, and in that cynical chuckle William caught an echo of Uncle Daniel himself. Bob's suggestion was excellent. With such a letter in their hands his parents would never have to fear Uncle Daniel's threats of lawyers.

Bob stayed with them until the coach was ready to leave. Waterloo Walter and Gentleman Joe greeted them with knowing smiles. 'Going to miss you,' said Bob, as she mounted the step.

She turned and looked down, lips parted in a smile. 'We are *cousins*,' she said and bent to kiss him. William sprang after her, Gentleman Joe sounded his bugle, and they were off.

The steep eastward road climbed into the sunrise. Gentleman Joe lifted his bugle again and played one of his favourite airs: *'Over the hills and far away!'*

EPILOGUE

'And where shall we go for this holiday?' asked William.

'It should be somewhere very special,' said Caroline. 'To celebrate your retirement – at last! And the first summer of the new century. And, if you haven't forgotten, our golden wedding.'

'Really?' he said teasingly.

'I know where I should like to go.'

'Where?'

'Redford!'

They had not been there since his mother's funeral twenty years ago. It would be good to see the place again, to walk the moors and dales while they still had the legs and lungs for it.

For old time's sake they took a room at the Coach and Horses, still a cosy welcoming inn but quieter than they had ever known it. The only coach was the one painted on the sign. There were horses in the stables still, but they were hunters and hacks and children's ponies. Redford was now a sleepy backwater. The railways had killed the coaching trade. There was no horn to sound at midnight – or any other time.

'That's the only horn now,' said William disgustedly. He pointed to one of the new-fangled motor-cars standing outside. A man in peaked cap and uniform was polishing its brasswork. Fixed on the side, close to the driver's hand, was a little horn to warn other traffic. It was sounded by squeezing an absurd rubber ball, when it emitted an unmusical *pap-pap!*

The innkeeper was at his elbow. 'Wonderful things, these motor-cars,' he said affably. 'If they catch on, folk won't have to go just where the railways take 'em!'

William bit his lip and thought silently of the railways he had helped to build, all over the world.

'With one of these,' said the landlord, 'you'll be able to go where you like, when you like.'

'But they'll never compete with the train,' said Caroline with a loyal squeeze of William's arm.

He could almost hear Waterloo Walter's confident voice of long ago. But he'd said the 'horse' not the 'train'.

'Maybe not, madam — but they might bring us a few more visitors, liven things up a bit.'

William could sympathize with the landlord. He remembered how the swift end of the mail-coaches had led to the decline in his father's business. Fred, of course, far-sighted and calculating, had got out in good time and gone off to become manager of a hideous redbrick railway hotel in one of the industrial cities.

'I'm all for progress myself,' said the landlord.

William could see his point. It would be wonderful if, somehow, this new invention could bring life back to the decaying country inns.

'Oh, so am I,' he agreed politely. 'All for progress.'

Was it fancy or was that Waterloo's sardonic chuckle from the grave?